Sonrise Stable
Carrie and Bandit

Vicki Watson

Illustrated by Becky Raber

Sonrise Stable Characters *(Horses in Parentheses)*

Grandma (Kezzie)

Lisa and Robert

Lauren

Kristy and Eric

Rosie *(Scamper)*

Carrie *(Bandit)*

Julie *(Elektra)* and Jonathan

Jared *(Scout)*
Jessie *(Patches)*
Jamie *(Pearl)*

Judy and Ross Robinson, foster parents

Barn cats: Katy and Jemimah

Thanks to Dr. Marylou Rings D.V.M, Rocky Knoll Large Animal Veterinary Services, for reviewing and offering suggestions for the veterinary scenes.

* Always wear a helmet when you ride. Helmets are not depicted in the illustrations for artistic purposes only.

Chapter 1

Bandit's New Home

Carrie turned in her seat, searching for Bandit's head through the small window in the horse trailer behind them. Thoughts swirled around in her mind, making her feel a little dizzy.

Eric laughed. "Is he still there, Carrie? I wouldn't want to lose him somewhere along the freeway."

Rosie twisted around and looked out the window. "He's still there and he's smashing Scamper up against the side of the trailer." She jabbed Carrie in the side with her elbow.

"It's not my fault. He must not be used to riding with other horses."

Carrie had a lot to get used to herself. Could she ever think of Eric and Kristy as her father and mother? It was easier to imagine Rosie as her sister. They had spent so much time together the past few years; they almost felt like sisters anyway.

Carrie was still processing the news she and Rosie had received a few days earlier: Rosie's parents wanted to adopt Carrie and make her a member of their family. It wouldn't be official until the court hearing in a few weeks, but then she would no longer be Carrie Rogers. She would be Carrie Jackson.

It was mid August and the girls were returning from the county fair, where they had spent the previous week showing Scamper and Kezzie. During the fair they had been horrified to find one of the exhibitors, Billy King, abusing his pony, Bandit. In order to rescue Bandit and surprise Carrie, Eric had purchased the pony. Since they lived in town, Bandit would stay at Grandma's farm, along with Scamper and Kezzie.

"There's Grandma's house!" Rosie announced as soon as she saw the Sonrise Stable sign, with its horse and cross, at the stable entrance.

"Pull up to the barn, Eric." Kristy retrieved her phone from the pocket of her jeans. "I'll let Mom know we're here."

Eric drove past the riding arena and parked the truck and trailer in front of the white stable. Jemimah, the barn cat, stared down at them from the hayloft door. The girls jumped out of the truck. Rosie's dark pigtails bobbed as she ran to open the tack area of the trailer. Her tanned skin was evidence of the many hours spent under the hot Ohio summer sun, working with her pony, Scamper. Both girls were ten, but Carrie was a few months younger. Although Carrie was blonde-haired, blue-eyed, and an inch shorter, after the adoption the girls hoped to convince people they were twins.

Carrie spotted Grandma walking down the path from the house to the barn. "We're here!"

"So I see! I have Bandit's stall ready for him. I think Scamper and Kezzie will like having another horse in the barn. I know I've been looking forward to his arrival. Let me get Kezzie out of the trailer."

Grandma opened the door of the maroon, four-horse trailer, attached a lead rope to Kezzie's halter, and unfastened the trailer tie. She rubbed Kezzie's forehead. "It's good to have you back, girl. Even though it was only a week, it sure felt strange with no horses in the barn."

Over the years, Grandma had boarded a few horses and given riding lessons at her farm, Sonrise Stable. Now she was enjoying retirement and her grandchildren. She had taught Rosie and Carrie to ride. They were not only becoming excellent riders, they also fed and cared for their horses, and helped with other barn chores.

Carrie backed Bandit out next. She stared at the pony. His golden coat glowed in the sunshine. *Is he really mine?* Riding at Sonrise Stable the past two years, she had grown to love horses nearly as much as Rosie and couldn't believe she actually had one of her own now. Maybe she would wake up to find that she wasn't going to be adopted after all and she hadn't received a pony of her own.

Rosie stepped into the trailer and snapped a lead rope onto Scamper's halter. While Carrie waited for Rosie to unload her pony, she closed her eyes and pinched herself on the arm. Slowly, she opened one eye. Yes, Bandit was still there, standing beside her.

Eric came around the side of the trailer. "Do you need any—"

Bandit startled and leaped sideways, nearly knocking Carrie over. As she scrambled to get out of his way, her boots slid on the loose gravel. She fell, but managed to hold on to the lead rope. "Whoa, boy! What's the matter?" Carrie held firmly to the lead as she got back on her feet.

"What are you afraid of?" Bandit turned and snorted, showing the whites of his eyes.

"Are you okay?" Grandma bent down and brushed the dust off Carrie's jeans. "He's probably a little fearful of men, since he was mistreated by his previous owner. It will take some time to gain his trust."

Carrie looked down at a small tear in the knee of her jeans. "My hand's a little sore, but I held on," she said proudly.

Eric approached the pony cautiously. "Don't be afraid of me, buddy. I'm the one who saved you, remember?" Eric didn't ride much, but he loved animals, especially horses. Bandit held his head high and eyed him suspiciously. Eric turned sideways, in a less threatening position, and let Bandit sniff his hand. He stroked the pony's neck and then moved away. "I'll take it gradually with him, until he learns to trust me."

Bandit dropped his head and nudged Carrie's arm. "Where do you want him, Grandma?" she asked.

"Put him in the middle stall. That will allow him to get acquainted with both Scamper and Kezzie." Grandma led Kezzie into the third stall, toward the back of the barn.

"You get the first stall because you're the best!" Rosie said to her pony, Scamper, a black-and-white pinto. Carrie gave her a look, but was too busy with Bandit to argue. Rosie removed Scamper's halter, closed his door, and latched it. The pony turned around twice and then lay down in a large pile of soft pine shavings.

Kristy leaned against the stall door and looked down at Scamper. "That's how I feel too after a week of fair—exhausted!"

"How much should I feed Bandit?" Carrie asked. Although she was not legally her granddaughter yet, Grandma had long ago insisted that Carrie call her "Grandma," and neither could imagine it any other way. Carrie was shy around people she didn't know well and sometimes couldn't think of the right thing—or anything—to say, but when the conversation involved horses, she was more comfortable. Rosie was the easiest for her to talk to. Although Carrie was only a few months younger, she looked up to Rosie in many ways as the older sister.

"Give them each two flakes of hay and a scoop of grain," Grandma directed.

Rosie and Carrie worked together feeding and watering all three horses, then Carrie turned a bucket upside-down outside Bandit's stall and stood on it to watch him eat. "I still can't believe you're mine." She looked over Bandit, trying to memorize every detail about him. He was a striking palomino, with a gleaming golden coat, wide blaze, and four white stockings. His mane and tail were dazzlingly white. Standing a little over fourteen hands, he was just two inches shy of being a horse. Most people would not realize that he was, in fact, a pony.

Carrie looked over at Rosie. "Who do you think is prettier? Bandit or Scamper?"

"That's a dumb question. Of course Scamper is prettier."

"Well, I think Bandit is prettier."

"Nope! No way."

"I can see having two daughters is going to be interesting," Kristy laughed. "Since they are both geldings, I doubt that either of them would want to be called 'pretty.' I'd say they're both handsome in their own way, just like you two are both beautiful in your own way. Does that work?"

Carrie and Rosie laughed, but it was obvious each was convinced her own horse was the nicest looking.

Eric looked over Carrie's shoulder at Bandit. "He looks content, don't you think?"

Carrie nodded, but didn't reply, still feeling a bit shy around Eric.

"Okay, girls," he said. "I'm going to unhook the trailer, then we need to head for home. Kris, would you mind giving me a hand?"

"Can I run over real quick to say 'Hi' to the Robinsons?" Carrie asked.

"Sure, but don't be too long. We need to leave soon," Kristy said as she followed Eric toward the truck.

Carrie and Rosie ran out of the barn and across the pasture to the neighbors, Judy and Ross Robinson, who had been Carrie's foster parents for the past two years.

Eric watched through the rear view mirror as Grandma waved her hand, signaling him to back the trailer into the gravel parking area.

Grandma held up her hand. "That's far enough."

Kristy popped the trailer latch open and began cranking the hitch to raise it high enough for Eric to pull the truck out. By the time they had the trailer unhooked, the girls were running back across the field.

"That didn't take long," Grandma remarked.

"I told them everything about Bandit." Carrie paused and caught her breath. "And that I'd be back tomorrow to see them again."

"Yes, we'll try to get over here once a day now. We don't want to make extra work for Mom."

"You mean at my age? I'm not over the hill yet, you know!" Grandma replied.

Kristy laughed. "That's not what I meant and you know it, Mom. I don't think you'll ever slow down. I just want the girls to be responsible for their own horses."

Carrie and Rosie were excited about seeing their grandmother and their horses every day.

"Since you're being adopted, you'll be homeschooled too," Rosie said.

"I hadn't thought of that!" Carrie replied. She didn't have any close friends at school and had often been envious of the free time Rosie had.

"Yes, my class will double in size this year." Kristy smiled.

"Make sure you come tomorrow. I'll have a surprise for you," Grandma announced.

"A surprise? What is it?" Carrie asked.

"Yeah, what kind of surprise?" Rosie asked. Carrie chimed in and they begged, "Please, tell us!"

Grandma just smiled. "You'll find out tomorrow," was all she would say.

Chapter 2

The Surprise

"Mom, don't ever do that to me again," Kristy groaned as she walked through the front door of Grandma's house the next morning. "These two woke me up at five o'clock wondering if we could come over right away. It was pitch-black outside!"

"Come on in. I'm just finishing a cup of coffee."

Rosie pushed ahead of Carrie and rushed into the kitchen. "What's the surprise, Grandma?"

Carrie ran to catch up with her. "Yeah, we can't stand it any longer."

Grandma smiled mysteriously and slowly rinsed her cup in the sink. "Follow me out to the barn and I'll show you."

"Oh Mom, you didn't buy another horse, did you?" Kristy stared at her mother with a questioning look.

The girl's eyes grew wide. Rosie tugged at her grandmother's sleeve. "Did you get another horse, Grandma? Did you?"

"Oh, I bet that's it!" Carrie looked up at Grandma. "What kind is it?"

Grandma looked from Rosie to Carrie and smiled. She marched through the living room toward the back door and motioned for them to follow. The girls danced around the adults as they walked down the gravel path to the barn. The horses hadn't been fed yet, and they nickered eagerly when they saw the group approaching.

"I bet it's an Icelandic," Rosie whispered to Carrie. "I've heard Grandma say she always wanted an Icelandic."

"Maybe it's a Friesian. Those horses are beautiful!" Carrie said.

The girls ran ahead and pushed the big sliding barn door open. They looked around expectantly, but were surprised when they didn't see any horses other than Scamper, Bandit, and Kezzie.

"Hi Bandit, I missed you, buddy," Carrie called out to her new horse.

Grandma walked past the horses' stalls toward the tack room at the back of the barn.

"What is that?" Carrie asked. The girls stopped and listened. From the direction of the tack room a soft whimper increased until it became a loud crowing.

"What is it, Grandma? A sick rooster?" Rosie frowned. "That's not a very good surprise."

Grandma opened the tack room door with a flourish, and a roly-poly ball of black fur burst through and launched herself at Rosie. The puppy fell to the ground and began pulling on the laces of Rosie's boots. "Hey, let go of my boots!" Wiggling with delight, the little black ball bounced back and forth between the two girls, her tongue moving as rapidly as her stump of a tail.

Rosie watched the pup lick Carrie's arm. "She thinks you need a bath, Carrie."

Carrie grabbed the squirmy pup and hugged her. "She's so soft! I love her! Look at the little brown spots above her eyes. She's adorable."

"All right, what's up with this, Mom?" Kristy stooped down and joined the girls in lavishing attention on the newest resident of Sonrise Stable.

"A friend of mine had a Rottweiler who was expecting a litter of pups. She knew I hadn't had a dog since Tess died, so she saved the pick of the litter for me. Isn't she cute?"

The pup jumped up and licked Carrie on the mouth. "Yech!" Carrie wiped away the slobbers with the back of her hand.

"You're going to have to help me teach her some manners." Grandma gently but firmly corrected the pup, making her sit still, if only for a second. "She doesn't have a name yet. Do you have any ideas?"

"I know! Duchess," Rosie suggested. "I've always liked that name. Or how about Midnight?"

"I like Roxie," added Carrie. "Roxie the Rottweiler."

Kristy pointed toward Scamper, who had his head over the stall door watching them. "Why don't you think of more names while you're feeding the horses?"

"Aww, Mom, you just want the puppy all to yourself," Rosie whined. She and Carrie kissed the pup on the head and started their chores.

Scamper banged his feed bucket against the wall. "He's saying, 'Feed me first!'" Rosie laughed.

Grandma shook her head and sighed. "Wait until he stops banging his bucket, then feed him. We don't want to reward his bad behavior."

"She's going to be a beautiful dog," Kristy said. The pup sat down on her foot and stared up at her. "How big do you think she'll get?"

"I'd guess about the same size as her mother. She weighs ninety pounds"

"You're going to be a good watchdog, aren't you?" The pup cocked her head sideways as if considering what Kristy had said.

"How about Fudge?" Rosie shouted, pushing a bale of hay down from the hay mow.

"Or Tootsie Roll?" Carrie suggested.

A big grin came over Kristy's face. "What about Tick?"

"Tick?" Rosie gave her mother a puzzled look. "What kind of name is that for a dog?"

"She's going to be a watch-dog, isn't she? You know—tick tock."

The girls groaned and went back to finish caring for the horses.

"It says in Revelation that one day we'll all be given new names,[1]" Grandma said.

"I'm going to have a new name," Carrie said as she stood outside Bandit's stall watching him eat. "Pretty soon I'll be Carrie Jackson!"

"That's right. It won't be too much longer now. You know who else needs a new name?"

Carrie looked at Grandma blankly. "No, who?"

"I think you should give your horse a new name. I'm not crazy about 'Bandit.' It sounds like a bank robber. Besides it will make him feel special, like he's being adopted too. In a way he is, because he has you for an owner now, a new home, and Scamper and Kezzie as his brother and sister."

Carrie smiled. "I never thought about it that way, but it is like being adopted. What do you think, Bandit? Would you like a new name?" The pony raised his head from the feed bucket and stared at Carrie, then went back to eating. "He says it's all right with him," Carrie announced.

"So," Kristy said, "we'll have three new names. One is already decided, but two we need to pick out. If you girls are finished, why don't you go play with Little-Miss-What's-Her-Name while Grandma and I talk?"

---

[1] He who has an ear, let him hear what the Spirit says to the churches. To him who overcomes I will give some of the hidden manna to eat. And I will give him a white stone, and on the stone a new name written which no one knows except him who receives it. Revelation 2:17

The girls took off running toward a grassy hill in front of the barn. When they looked back, they saw the pup sitting at Grandma's feet, staring at them. Carrie turned around and clapped her hands. "Come on, girl, you can come with us."

Grandma gave her a nudge, and the puppy took off so fast she lost her balance and fell, nearly turning a somersault. Carrie flipped her right-side-up again, and the girls slowed down so she could keep up with them.

The adults walked over to the picnic table. "Is everything okay, honey? You look a little worried." Grandma sat down beside her daughter.

"Oh Mom." Kristy looked as if she were about to burst into tears. "Eric hasn't had much work lately. It seems no one is interested in building houses these days. We're having a hard time keeping up with our bills."

Grandma immediately felt a sharp, painful sensation that only a parent would understand. She remembered the days when her daughters were young, and they came to her with problems small enough for her to solve. Now the solutions did not come so easily. "Oh, Kris, I wish I had the money to help you."

"Oh no, I wouldn't ask you for that." Kristy waved away her mother's suggestion. "I've renewed my sign language certification, and I'm going to be on call as an interpreter at the hospital. I would feel much better if I knew I could drop the kids off here whenever I have an appointment."

"Well, *that* I can do! I'll be glad to watch them."

"I may not be able to give you much notice since some will be emergency appointments. I'll send their books along so they don't get behind. They can work together on most of their assignments. I hate to have them just working from textbooks, but that's going to have to do for now."

"I'm here most of the time anyway, so that won't be a problem. It will be like old times, when I was homeschooling you and your sisters." Grandma smiled. "I enjoyed those years so much. Well, most of it! I guess we did have a few rough days once in a while."

"I wouldn't trade those times for the world." Kristy gave her mother a hug.

"Do you have a date for the adoption hearing yet?"

"Oh, I forgot to tell you. It's September eighth, about three weeks away. I haven't told the girls yet, but Lisa and Lauren are flying up from Texas. I guess Robert couldn't get time off from work.

"It will mean a lot to Carrie to have them here," Grandma said. "I'm so excited I can hardly wait! I can't imagine how Carrie must feel."

Carrie overheard the last part of the conversation and wandered over to the picnic table. "How I must feel about what?"

"About your adoption day," Grandma said. "Are you as excited as I am?"

Carrie paused for a moment. "I'm excited, but a little nervous. I don't know what's going to happen."

Rosie came over to join the others, the puppy in her arms. "Wow, she's heavy!" She shifted the pup from her left side to her right. "What *does* happen when you get adopted, Mom?"

"Rosie, put the dog down." Grandma said. "She'll be way too big to carry around real soon."

Carrie looked expectantly at Kristy.

"Oh, about the adoption—the way I understand it we'll meet with the judge, our attorney, and the social worker at the courthouse. The judge will ask us some questions and then we'll sign the legal papers."

"That doesn't sound too bad." Carrie looked relieved. "Grandma, can I ride Bandit today?"

"Maybe later tonight. Julie is coming over and I want her to ride him first to make sure he's okay before you ride him the first time."

"Is she bringing Jamie and Jessie? They have to see the puppy!" Rosie said.

"Yes. Jared's at a friend's house, but the twins will be here. I think tonight would be the perfect time to settle on a name for the pup. I'm already tired of calling her 'pup.'"

"They can give me some ideas for Bandit's new name too," Carrie said. "I'm going to go clean his stall." Grandma held the puppy so she wouldn't go into the barn around the horses. The girls grabbed two pitchforks, tossed them into the wheelbarrow, and parked it between the stalls.

Carrie picked up her pitchfork and started toward Bandit's stall. "I still can't believe I have my own horse."

"I think you've said that at least a hundred times now." Rosie rolled her eyes. "Do you want me to pinch you this time, so you'll know you're not dreaming?"

"Umm, that won't be necessary! I think I just need to feel his soft coat again." Pitchfork in hand, Carrie slid the door open and stepped into the stall. Startled, Bandit whirled around and slammed into the wall with a loud thud. Carrie jumped back, tripped, and fell into the aisle.

Kristy leaped up from the picnic table and ran into the barn. "What happened, Carrie? Are you okay?" She leaned down and grabbed Carrie's arm, helping her back to her feet.

"I'm fine. I don't know what happened." Carrie brushed her jeans off. Her face clouded over, and she was on the verge of tears. "As soon as I started to go into the stall, Bandit got really scared and tried to run away. I don't think he likes me."

"Don't worry, Carrie," Grandma said. "I don't think it has anything to do with you—more likely it's that pitchfork you had in your hand. From his reaction, I'd say Bandit might have been hit with one by Billy." Grandma bent down and picked up the pitchfork. She tossed it aside angrily. Few things made Grandma as mad as people abusing animals.

Carrie remembered how angry she and Rosie had been when they had seen Billy whipping Bandit behind the horse tent at the fair. She peeked through the stall door. "You don't have to be afraid of me, Bandit."

Grandma quietly entered the stall, talking gently to Bandit and checking him to make sure he hadn't injured himself. "We'll let the three of them out in the pasture and you can clean the stalls then. Carrie, you take Kezzie and I'll lead Bandit."

Once the stalls were cleaned, Grandma turned to Kristy. "Can you spare these two for the rest of the day? I need some help putting up a pen for the puppy so I can keep her away from the horses. I'd sure hate to see her get stepped on."

Rosie and Carrie looked hopefully at Kristy.

"I suppose I can do without them for one day."

"Yay!" they both yelled. The puppy wasn't sure what the excitement was all about, but she joined in the fun, barking and running in circles.

"Okay. I'll be back in time to watch Julie ride." Kristy hugged the girls. "Don't forget you're supposed to be helping Grandma, not playing with the puppy. See you all later."

Chapter 3

Riding Bandit

Grandma pointed. "Bring me that long side panel." She and the girls were in the back yard, assembling an old dog kennel that had been stowed away behind the garage. The panel was long and awkward, but not too heavy.

"Get on the other side of it," Rosie directed. Carrie dropped her end, causing Rosie to lose her grip. The panel fell on her foot. "Ow! I didn't say drop it!"

"Sorry! I was just trying to do what you told me." Carrie hurried to pick her end up again.

"Okay, hold it up right here while I connect this end," Grandma said. With Grandma supervising and the girls carrying the pieces, it wasn't long until they had a nice, secure pen to contain the puppy when no one was able to supervise her.

Grandma scooped up the pup, who had worn herself out and was napping peacefully under a shady tree. She walked toward the front door. "It's time for her to be introduced to June Bug."

"Oh no—don't let her hurt the puppy, Grandma," Rosie said nervously.

June Bug, a stocky, bobtailed calico cat, was the queen of the house. She had all her claws and didn't hesitate to use them. In her grumpier moments, she still frightened Rosie and Carrie. Grandma set the puppy down in the entry. Hearing the commotion, it wasn't long before June Bug sauntered over to investigate. She froze when she spotted the pup. The hair on the back of her neck stood straight up, and her little stump of a tail poofed out. She growled and gave a warning hiss. The puppy kept her distance and barked at the cat.

"Looks like she may have already learned a lesson about tangling with a cat." Grandma laughed at the pair. "They just need some time to get acquainted."

Rosie watched the two animals eyeing each other. "Maybe it will be good for June Bug to have someone she can't beat up on."

June Bug continued to growl and slowly retreated, never turning her back on the pup. She jumped up onto the windowsill where she could watch the intruder.

"I don't know about you two, but I'm as hungry as a bear," Grandma said. She washed her hands in the kitchen sink and began to prepare lunch. The girls sat down in the entry. Carrie held the pup on her lap, stroking her sleek coat. The puppy's eyelids drooped, and she was soon asleep again. After a while, Rosie pulled the limp, sleepy pup onto her lap.

As Grandma busied herself in the kitchen the aroma of lunch drifted into the entryway. "Mmm, that smells good," Carrie said. "I'm starved."

"Go wash the puppy germs off your hands, and we'll eat," Grandma announced. She set out a plate of grilled cheese sandwiches and a pot of steaming vegetable soup.

Rosie sat down at the table. "Grilled cheese, my favorite!"

"Would you like to pray?" Grandma asked.

"Sure," Rosie replied. They all bowed their heads. "Heavenly Father, thank you so much for Grandma, and the new puppy, and—aaagh!" Rosie screeched and jumped up out of her chair, sending it flying over backwards with a loud crash. A blur of calico ran from the kitchen. The puppy was jarred out of a sound sleep and ran around the table barking. Grandma's eyes flew open, and she and Carrie both leaped to their feet.

"What is it? What's the matter?" Grandma rushed over to Rosie, who was wincing and turning a bit red.

"I'm okay," she said sheepishly. "I think June Bug was trying to scratch on the back of my chair, and she stuck her claws into my bottom." Rosie patted the injured area with her hand. She picked up the chair and sat down gingerly. Grandma and Carrie returned to their seats, staring intently at their plates, trying hard to remain serious, but first one, and then the other burst into laughter.

"It's not funny." Rosie frowned, but soon she was laughing along with them.

"Lord, thank You that we never have a dull moment around here. We ask Your blessing on this food. Amen." Grandma passed the sandwiches around. "Let's eat before it gets cold."

Rosie kept glancing nervously behind her to make sure June Bug didn't return.

"Mmmm, this is good, Grandma. Do you think I'll be able to ride Bandit tonight?" Carrie asked eagerly in between bites.

"If he does all right for Julie, I don't see why not."

"I have a great idea!" Rosie nearly jumped out of her chair again.

"What is this great idea?" Grandma replied.

"We should go on a trail ride to celebrate Carrie's adoption day!"

"Well, the adoption is in the afternoon. We'd have to do it the day after," Grandma mused. "That would give Carrie a few weeks to get comfortable riding Bandit. Sounds like a good plan to me. I'll even get to ride my own horse." She smiled at Carrie.

"I still can't believe—"

Rosie reached out and put her hand over Carrie's mouth. "Yes, you have your own horse! Please stop saying that!"

"Nf tho nmbe—" Carrie mumbled behind Rosie's hand.

"Rosie, take your hand off her," Grandma insisted. "What was that, Carrie?"

"I said, 'I'm so happy!' I've never had any animal of my own before, let alone a horse."

"It will take you two a while to get to know each other, but I think you'll do fine with him," Grandma assured her.

After helping clean the kitchen, the girls went to the barn to wait for Julie. They called the horses to the fence to feed them a few apples.

When Bandit saw Kezzie and Scamper eating, he approached the fence. Kezzie laid her ears back and charged at him, driving him away from the girls.

"Kezzie! Why are you being mean to Bandit?" Carrie stared at Kezzie in disbelief. "Why is she acting like that? She's usually so friendly."

"She's trying to prove she's the lead mare," Rosie explained. "They have a pecking order. Grandma told me all about it. I think Kezzie wants to make sure Bandit knows he's at the bottom."

Carrie walked down the fence row to where her horse had been banished and offered him an apple. "I bet you can't wait either." She patted his neck. "Tonight I'm going to ride you."

"He looks real excited about it," Rosie laughed. "Come on." She waved Carrie toward the barn. "Let's rearrange the tack room."

"Why?" Carrie asked.

"Well, as a horse owner, you have responsibilities now," Rosie said in her best imitation of her mother's voice. "Besides, we dumped all our stuff in there after the fair, so it's a mess."

"Like your room, you mean?"

"Hey, my room's not that bad. I'm just not a neat freak like you are."

The girls removed the saddles and saddle racks and swept the floor of the tack room. "Let's put your saddle beside mine," Rosie suggested.

Carrie dragged her saddle rack beside Rosie's and placed her saddle on it. They hung their bridles on the wall behind the saddles. The girls grabbed the dusty, dirty saddle blankets and carried them outside, draping them over the gate.

"Here, see if you can get it clean with this." Rosie tossed Carrie a horse brush.

"Next year I want to get a green saddle blanket to go with my show shirt." Carrie brushed the blanket, sending dust flying.

Rosie frowned. "Green looked good on Kezzie, but I don't know about Bandit. Besides, you'll probably outgrow that shirt by next summer anyway. I've been outgrowing all my clothes lately. Mom says I'm having a growth spurt." Since Rosie had been small for most of her childhood, she was glad to finally be catching up with the other kids her own age.

Carrie looked disappointed. Green was her favorite color. "What color would look good on a palomino?"

"I don't know. You should ask Mom. You can use any color but purple. That's my color." Rosie paused and stared at the blankets. "We're not getting these very clean. I think Mom will have to wash them." They took the blankets back inside, then dumped the brushes out of the grooming tub, cleaned each of them, and placed them back in an orderly way.

Julie poked her head into the tack room.

"You're here, Aunt Julie!" Rosie and Carrie jumped up.

"I didn't hear you pull in," Rosie said.

"I parked over at the house. Had to see the new puppy! Jessie and Jamie are bringing her over. What have you two been up to?" She looked around the tack room. "This place hasn't looked this good in a long time!"

The twins appeared in the doorway behind their mother. "You've held her long enough. It's my turn now," Jamie whined.

"Just a few more minutes," Jessie insisted. She turned away from her sister and squeezed the puppy so hard she yelped.

"You're hurting her. Give her to me! Mom, make Jessie give me the puppy."

"If you two don't stop fighting over her, I'm going to send you both back to the house. She's too big to carry around anyway. Put her down and take her out front, away from the horses. Rosie, why don't you get Scamper out and ride with me?"

Rosie grinned. "I was hoping you'd say that." She handed Bandit's halter and lead rope to her aunt and picked up Scamper's.

"Carrie, you catch Kezzie. We'll put her in her stall while we're riding the other two."

The girls walked right up to Kezzie and Scamper in the pasture and slipped their halters on. Bandit stayed back, apart from the other two. Julie walked between the horses and slowly approached him. When she got within a few feet of him, he whirled away and galloped around the field.

"Bandit, come back!" Carrie called.

"You little monkey." Julie sighed and dropped her hands to her sides. "Go ahead and take those two into the barn," she directed. "This might take a while."

The girls led the horses through the gate and closed it behind them. Carrie looked back at her aunt. "Do you want some grain, Aunt Julie?"

"No. Not yet, anyway. I might try that later if I get desperate."

Suddenly, Bandit noticed that his friends had left him. He stopped, raised his head, and looked in their direction. He wanted to join them, but Julie was standing between him and the gate. He took off running again.

Carrie led Kezzie into her stall and latched the door. She turned slowly around and picked up a brush to help Rosie groom Scamper.

"What's going on?" Grandma asked as she arrived at the barn. "You look like you just lost your best friend, Carrie."

"Bandit's being a bad boy. He won't let Aunt Julie catch him."

"Well, he doesn't know who he's tangling with," Grandma said. "You two get Scamper ready. I'll see if she needs any help."

Carrie halfheartedly brushed Scamper while Rosie picked his hooves. "Do you think Bandit will ever be this friendly?"

"Sure he will. He just needs a little more time. He hasn't even been here two full days yet," Rosie encouraged her.

Grandma walked over to the pasture gate and leaned against it. "Need any help?" she yelled out to Julie.

"Nah, he's just testing me. He doesn't realize yet how much smarter I am." Julie looked around. "You have a lot of branches out here that need picked up." She whistled to herself, stooping to pick up branches and carrying them over to a growing pile.

"I appreciate the help cleaning up, but what in the world are you doing? That's a strange way to catch a horse."

Julie smiled. "Just watch."

She ignored Bandit, who was beginning to tire of running around the field. He seemed to have expected her to chase him and looked surprised when she didn't. He stopped at a distance and stared at her. Julie glanced at him briefly and returned to picking up sticks.

Bandit's curiosity got the best of him. He approached the pile of sticks and sniffed. Julie calmly patted him on the neck and walked away. Bandit watched her as she left. Julie walked up to the gate and talked with Grandma for a while. Soon Bandit came up to investigate. She petted him again and turned back to her mother.

"I think you could catch him now," Grandma said, still confused by Julie's approach.

"My goal isn't to 'catch' him," Julie explained. "I want him to feel comfortable coming up to me. It will take a lot of time to completely cure him of this habit. He's not a bad horse. He was afraid of Billy, so he learned to run away from him. We need to develop a relationship so he wants to be with us."

After a while, Julie placed the lead rope around Bandit's neck, gently slipped the halter onto his head and led him toward the barn.

Grandma followed. "You're good at that. I get too impatient. That's one thing that really annoys me—a horse I can't catch."

"Aunt Julie, how am I going to ride my horse if I can't even catch him?" Carrie complained.

"Imagine it from his perspective, Carrie. If every time Billy got him out he mistreated him, how excited do you think Bandit is about being caught and ridden?"

"But I haven't been mean to him," Carrie said. "And I won't ever be."

"You and I know that, but Bandit doesn't realize it yet. Give him some time, love, and patience, and he'll grow to trust you. That doesn't mean you should let him get away with bad behavior, though. He'll understand the difference between being corrected for doing something wrong and just plain meanness."

"Are you sure?" Carrie asked.

"Guaranteed. Now, why don't you help me brush him? Just don't make any sudden, unexpected movements."

Carrie ran a brush through Bandit's long mane. "Do you have any ideas for a new name for him, Aunt Julie?"

"Hmmm, I really don't like the name, 'Bandit.' Reminds me of a burglar or thief."

"That's what I was thinking too," Grandma agreed, "but I haven't come up with any good ideas."

"What about Golden Boy?" Rosie asked.

"That's a nice name, but it seems like every palomino I know is named Gold Something-or-Other," Julie said. "Maybe we could come up with something unique."

Kristy entered the barn. "You mean like Tick, the watch-dog?"

"Hi Mom!" Rosie said.

"Looks like I'm just in time."

"Yep, we're about ready. He was a bit difficult to catch, but he seems okay now." Julie went to the tack room and returned with Grandma's saddle. "You know, Carrie, a bandit is someone who takes things from people." She placed the saddle on Bandit's back. "Maybe we could come up with a name that has to do with giving instead."

"I think he'll give Carrie a lot of joy. Remember Joy? She was the first horse we had when you kids were young, even before Ebony." Grandma frowned. "But I suppose 'Joy' doesn't work very well for a gelding."

"She wasn't much of a joy to ride," Kristy said. "I couldn't kick her hard enough to get her to move."

"How about Santa?" Rosie piped up. "He's supposed to give toys to children."

Carrie stomped her foot and frowned at Rosie. "I am not going to name my horse Santa."

"How about Nate? Like in do-nate?" Julie said.

"I've got it! I've got it!" Carrie squealed and jumped up and down.

Everyone stopped what they were doing and stared at her.

"What?" Grandma asked.

"Zacchaeus!" Carrie said, as if it should have been perfectly obvious to everyone.

"Well, Bandit *is* short—for a horse, anyway," Grandma agreed. She began singing, "Zacchaeus was a wee little man…"

"It's more than that," Carrie said excitedly. "Don't you remember the story we read in Sunday school a few weeks ago, Rosie?"

"Oh yeah," Rosie said. "When Zacchaeus met Jesus, he agreed to give half his money to the poor and to pay back ten times what he had cheated people out of."

Grandma smiled. "I think it was four times, Rosie."

"We can call him 'Zach,' for short," Carrie said.

"That's perfect, Carrie! Why didn't I think of that?" Julie pulled the girth strap snug. "Okay, Zach, you need a new attitude to go with your new name. No more tricks from you." She led the pony out of the barn. Rosie followed Julie out to the arena on Scamper.

"Do whatever you normally do, Rosie. I'm going to start Zach off slowly."

Julie walked Zach around the arena a few times, allowing him to get used to the new surroundings. She turned and backed him. "He neck reins really well," she remarked to Carrie who was perched on the arena fence watching her pony's every move. Julie trotted and cantered. After she had worked him thoroughly in both directions, she stopped in front of Carrie. Rosie came up and stood beside them on Scamper.

33

Julie smiled and hopped down. "Carrie, he's a dream to ride. Smooth, and responsive to the slightest touch on the reins. I'd say you'll give Rosie some competition at the shows next summer."

Rosie frowned and patted Scamper's neck. "Don't worry, boy. We won't let them beat us, will we?"

"But, Kristy," Julie said, "next time Eric decides to buy a horse, have him talk to me—*before* he buys it, not after!"

Kristy smiled. "I don't think he's planning to buy any more horses, but I'll let him know."

"Can I ride him now?" Carrie looked anxiously from Kristy to Julie to Grandma.

"I don't think he'll give you any trouble under saddle. It only seems to be on the ground that he has a few issues, and those should disappear once he knows he can trust us," Julie said.

"Run and get your saddle. Mine is a little too big for you," Grandma said.

Carrie sprinted for the barn.

"That's one happy girl," Kristy remarked. "Thanks so much for keeping Ban—I mean Zacchaeus—for us, Mom."

"Oh, one more horse isn't that much trouble."

Carrie returned with her saddle on her hip, grinning from ear to ear. "Seeing that smile on her face is more than worth it," Grandma said.

Julie swapped the saddles and held Zach while Carrie mounted. The girls rode off together, chattering excitedly.

"Don't ride them side by side all the time," Julie instructed. "Separate them once in a while so they don't become too dependent on each other. Just walk and trot today, Carrie—we'll work on cantering another time."

"Reminds me of a few years ago when I was watching you two out there," Grandma said.

"That was more than a few years ago," Kristy laughed. "I sure wish Rosie and Carrie could grow up in the country."

"So they could jump out of the hayloft like we used to?" Julie asked.

"No, I was thinking more of the fun we had with all the animals."

"Oh, you mean the geese we raised from babies that turned into monsters that chased and attacked us when they were full grown?"

"The best part was chasing the cows when they got out. For some reason it seemed they always made their escape at the crack of dawn. I remember them trampling all over the neighbor's yard and running through his garden. I bet he celebrated when Dad finally sold all of them," Kristy said.

Grandma smiled at the memories. "The girls are welcome to spend as much time with me as you want them to. It can get a little lonely around here. Tick will be some company, but she's not much of a conversationalist.

Speaking of that, where did that dog go?" Grandma looked around. "Looks like the twins are gone too."

"I bet I know where they are. Keep an eye on Carrie. I'll be right back." Julie jogged past the barn, scrambled down the ravine, and found Jessie and Jamie at their favorite spot by the creek, skipping rocks and laughing as Tick ran back and forth along the edge of the water, barking at the splashes.

"When she gets a little bigger, she'll probably be *in* the creek. Our dog, Tess, loved swimming on hot days," Julie remembered. "Come back up to the arena, girls. We won't be too much longer, and you can watch Carrie ride."

The twins raced back to the arena and climbed up on the fence. "You look great!" Jamie yelled encouragingly to Carrie as she watched her trot Zach in a figure eight.

"Yeah, a lot better than you and Pearl," Jessie said. Jamie made a face at her sister. After they had ridden a few more laps, Carrie and Rosie rode over to the twins.

"Hey, we're going on a trail ride to celebrate Carrie's adoption day," Rosie said. "Why don't you ask your mom if you can come with us?"

"Sounds like fun." Jamie called out to her mother, "Mom, can we go on a trail ride with Rosie and Carrie?"

"Grandma mentioned that. I'd love to, but aren't you forgetting something? We have fair that week. We'll have to do it another time."

"Oh yeah, forgot about that," Jamie said.

"You'll have to come and watch us show at the fair," Jessie said.

"Yeah, we will," Rosie and Carrie agreed.

"Okay, let's put them up now," Julie said. "I need to get home and feed my horses."

"And us!" Jessie said. "I'm hungry."

Julie patted Carrie's shoulder. "You were great today. I'll come back a few more times this week to help you. Before long, you'll be as comfortable on old Zacchaeus here as you are on Kezzie."

Chapter 4

Creek Crossing

"So you're starting your homeschooling early this year?" Grandma asked, looking through the books Rosie and Carrie were pulling out of their backpacks. Kristy had dropped them off early that morning on her way to an emergency appointment at the hospital.

"Yes, Mom doesn't want us to get behind. And she said we're not allowed to even look at the horses until our school work is done. I don't think that's fair," Rosie complained.

"Sounds fair to me. She must have learned that from her teacher when she was young," Grandma said with a grin.

Rosie could see that she wasn't going to get any sympathy from her grandmother. "Carrie and I are going to work together since she's never been homeschooled before. We're in the same grade, and we're going to be twins next week," Rosie said.

"So I hear," Grandma laughed. "Let me know if you need any help."

"Can we do math first?" Carrie asked. "I don't like it, and I like to do things I don't like first to get them over with."

"Okay," Rosie agreed. She pulled her math book out and opened it to the first lesson. "This looks easy. I did this kind of problem last year. Let's see who can get done first."

The girls were absorbed in solving math problems while Grandma quietly tidied up the kitchen. Suddenly, there was a loud scratching and scraping sound followed by a thud. The girls' heads jerked up from their books. "Are you okay, Grandma?" They ran into the kitchen. "What happened?"

Grandma pointed to the corner. "I'm fine. It's that crazy cat. Watch."

The girls turned and saw June Bug sitting in the corner staring intently at a spot about four feet up on the wall. Before long, she sprang straight up in the air. Her claws scraped down the wall as she returned with a thud to the floor.

The girls laughed. "What is she doing?"

"At certain times of the day, the light casts a shadow from the light switch onto the wall in that corner of the kitchen," Grandma explained. "It drives her crazy. She never gives up trying to catch the evil thing."

"Your cat is really weird," Carrie said.

"She is rather peculiar. I think God sent her to me. I don't know anyone else who would put up with her." Grandma shook her head with a smile. "I left the puppy in her pen so she wouldn't distract you, but I forgot about June Bug. Open the door for me, girls." Grandma crept toward the corner and carefully picked up the cat. Rosie ran to open the door, and Grandma deposited June Bug on the porch. "Now you two get back to work!"

(from photo)

The girls finished their math and moved on to science. "Let me check your answers," Grandma said when they were done. "That will be one less thing your mom has to do tonight." When their work was completed to Grandma's satisfaction, she said, "Get your boots on and we'll head over to the barn."

Carrie packed her books into her backpack and started toward the laundry room to pick up her riding boots. As she passed Grandma's bedroom, a bright red plastic bag caught her eye. The bag looked as if it had been hastily tossed onto the bed in Grandma's otherwise neat and orderly room.

I wonder what that is? Carrie glanced quickly behind her and quietly entered the room. The bag made, what seemed to Carrie, an extremely loud crinkling noise when she picked it up. She was certain for a moment that Grandma and Rosie would come rushing in to see what she was doing.

When no one appeared, she peeked in the bag and pulled out a small, white box. She turned the box over, studying it curiously, then carefully removed the lid. Inside was a silver, heart-shaped locket on a bed of soft, fluffy cotton. *Oh, it's beautiful.* A horse's head was etched on the front of the locket. She pried it open, but there was nothing inside.

She listened and heard Rosie and Grandma talking in the living room. Stepping over to the mirror, she held the locket up to her neck. A twinge of her conscience told her it was wrong, but she slipped the necklace into her pocket and started toward the door. Looking back over her shoulder, she saw the empty box and bag. She ran back, picked them up, and tossed them under the bed. Hurrying to the laundry room, she grabbed her boots and returned to the living room.

Carrie sat down and pulled her boots on. She felt as if Rosie and Grandma were staring right through her. As soon as both boots were on, she hopped up. "Beat you to the barn, Rosie!" She flew out the back door.

Caught off guard, Rosie took off after her, but didn't catch up until they reached the barn. "No fair, you had a head start!" The girls were breathing hard as they carried their equipment out of the tack room.

Grandma helped Carrie groom and saddle Zach, then she led Kezzie out of her stall.

"You're riding with us today?" Rosie asked.

"Yes, since Julie worked so much with Carrie and Zach last week, I thought we would ride through the woods and along the creek today. It will be good practice for our trail ride next week."

When they were all mounted, Grandma led the way on Kezzie. She turned to look at Carrie who was riding behind her. "You know what? I think I know how you feel."

"What?" She gulped. *How could Grandma know what I did?*

"I can't believe I have my own horse!" Grandma laughed. "It's nice to have Kezzie back."

"Oh, yeah," Carrie said weakly as Grandma turned back around. She stood in her stirrups and reached inside her jeans pocket to make sure the necklace was still there.

"Aw, I hear Tick crying." Rosie looked back toward the house. "Can't she go with us, Grandma?"

"No," Grandma insisted. "She's not smart enough to stay away from the horses yet. In a few more months we should be able to bring her along." Grandma dismounted and opened the gate to the back pasture. The horses were eager to enter the coolness of the woods.

"I can't wait till our trail ride." Rosie trotted Scamper to catch up with Grandma and Carrie. "Is Aunt Lisa coming with us?"

Grandma shook her head. "No, they're going to visit Robert's mother in the hospital before they return to Texas. It will just be your mom and me and the two of you. We'll have another whole-family trail ride during Cousins Camp next year."

"That was so much fun." Carrie thought about the weeklong camp they'd had with all the kids. They had been so new to her then, but they would soon be her real cousins. She forgot about the necklace for a while and concentrated on steering Zach down the path that wandered through the woods along the creek.

"Let's see how Zach likes water," Grandma said. "This is a good place to cross." The shallow, winding creek formed the back boundary of Grandma's property. The water was so clear you could see the rocks on the creek bed and schools of small fish busily swimming here and there. Kezzie and Scamper didn't hesitate as they stepped down into the water.

Zach, on the other hand, snorted and pawed and stopped to take a drink. Grandma watched him begin to paw again. "Pull his head up before he—jump off!" Grandma yelled.

"What?" Carrie suddenly felt Zach collapse underneath her. She leaped off and fell backwards into the water. The horse went down with a splash. He stretched his legs out in front of him and sighed.

Grandma jumped off Kezzie, sloshed through the water, and pulled Carrie up. She was soaked and a little scared, but unharmed.

"Are you okay, Carrie?" Rosie urged Scamper back across the creek. "Grandma, do you need any help?"

"You stay on Scamper," Grandma said. "One soaked girl is enough." She tugged on Zach's reins. He pulled back, lying contentedly in the water. Grandma pulled harder, and he rose up on his front legs, sitting up like a dog on his hindquarters.

"Come on," Grandma said. "Let's get out of this water." Zach stood all the way up and stepped up onto the bank.

Carrie came along behind them. "Eeeww, my boots are full of water." She pulled one off, turned it upside down, and watched dirty creek water spill out. She struggled to get the boot back on, then emptied the other one. Zach shook violently.

"Aaagh!" Carrie yelled as more muddy water splattered all over her. "What's wrong with him, Grandma? Is he sick or something?"

"No, I think he's fine. I should have seen the signs and warned you sooner. Some horses love to lay down in water, especially if they feel hot and itchy."

"Are you sure you're okay, Carrie?" Rosie asked.

Carrie nodded, wringing her shirt out with shaky hands. "Yeah, it was a little scary, but I'm okay."

"You better get inside and get some clean, dry clothes on," Grandma said. "If you're okay with it, I think you need to get back on now, though. I can lead you back to the barn. This horse is smart. If he thinks lying down in the water will get him out of work, he'll be likely to try it again next time."

Carrie stared at her pony doubtfully. Since he arrived, she seemed to have ended up on the ground nearly as often as she'd been on him. She was beginning to wonder what he might try next. If Grandma thought she needed to get back on, she'd give it a try. She patted his shoulder and lifted her leg toward the saddle. Her wet jeans were so stiff she couldn't bend her leg far enough to reach the stirrup.

Grandma helped her up, then remembered Kezzie. Turning around, she saw her standing in the middle of the creek, watching them with a puzzled expression. "You big goof, come over here." She clapped her leg and clucked for Kezzie to come. Kezzie stared at her, but didn't move. "Oh, all right. I guess I'm not going to get any wetter." Grandma handed Carrie Zach's reins and waded into the creek to retrieve her horse.

With Carrie and Zach on her right and Kezzie on her left, Grandma started back toward the barn, water squishing inside her boots with every step. Rosie rode on the other side of Carrie. "I have some extra clothes upstairs you can wear," she offered.

"Yes, throw your wet clothes in the basket in the laundry room, and I'll wash them later," Grandma said.

When they got back to the barn, they put the horses in their stalls. "You two go on over to the house and get cleaned up while I finish taking care of the horses," Grandma said.

Rosie stared at Carrie and burst into laughter. "You are a mess! You have mud all over your face and in your hair."

Carrie ran her fingers through her hair, then wiped them off on her jeans.

"Hop in the shower, Carrie," Grandma called after them as the girls started toward the house.

Grandma grabbed both sides of Zach's bridle and pulled his head close to her face. "What other tricks do you know?" she asked sternly. The pony nickered softly.

"Don't play innocent with me. Don't you know you could have hurt that little girl? If you want to stay here, you better behave yourself." She patted his shoulder and began to unsaddle him.

Grandma finished with the last horse and stepped out of the barn. She spotted Kristy's car coming down the road. By the time she reached the house, Carrie and Rosie were talking excitedly, both at the same time, telling Kristy about the adventure with Zach at the creek.

"I'm glad you weren't hurt, Carrie." Kristy gave her a hug. "Are you sure this horse is going to work out, Mom?"

Carrie looked anxiously toward Grandma.

"I think he'll be fine. It was partly my fault. I should have seen it coming sooner. We'll be more careful next time."

"I guess he just likes to go swimming," Carrie offered.

Kristy looked unconvinced. "Okay, if you're sure." She turned toward the girls. "I think we should get out of here so Grandma can have some peace and quiet. Carrie, what did you do with your wet clothes?"

"Oh, don't worry about those." Grandma waved her hand. "I have to wash mine too, so I'll throw them all in together."

"Thanks, Mom. I owe you." Kristy helped the girls gather their things.

"How was your appointment?" Grandma asked.

"It wasn't quite as exciting as your day, but everything went well. I need to go back tomorrow, if you feel up to having these two again."

"Sure. Although I think we'll just ride in the arena tomorrow."

After Kristy and the girls left, Grandma went to her bedroom to find some dry clothes. She stopped in the middle of the room and stared for a moment. *That's funny. I was sure I left Carrie's gift on the bed.* She looked around the room and in the closet. Pulling each dresser drawer open, she pawed through the clothing, but came up empty-handed. *Hmm—now, what could I have done with that bag?*

After excitedly rehashing every detail of Carrie's dip in the creek, the girls finally grew quiet on the trip home. Carrie stared out the car window, spotting the little restaurant around the corner from her new home. She sat back in her seat and closed her eyes. *I can't believe I'm being adopted. Thank you, God.* Suddenly, she remembered the necklace. She jammed her hand into her pocket and frantically searched for it, then tried the other pocket. Nothing. *Oh, no!* She realized she was wearing Rosie's old clothes. Her heart sank. *The necklace is in my jeans in Grandma's laundry room.*

Chapter 5

The Necklace

Eric held the front door open. "You're just in time. Pizza should be ready in five minutes. We're celebrating tonight!"

"Great, I'm starved," Rosie said. "What are we celebrating, Dad?" They all turned to look at Eric.

"I'll tell you during supper. Run and put your stuff away and we'll eat."

When they were gathered at the table, the family joined hands and Eric prayed.

"Let's hear your news first, then the girls have a story to tell you." Kristy placed slices of pizza on their plates.

"I got a new job today!" Eric announced.

"That's great, Dad!" Rosie said.

"You did!" Kristy exclaimed. "What kind of job?"

"Remember the apartment complex we built a few years ago? I ran into the owner at the bank today, and he mentioned that he was looking for a maintenance supervisor. It's a bit of a drive, and it won't pay as much as I was making before, but enough for us to live on. And you won't have to work as much, or at all, if you don't want to."

"Oh Eric, that's wonderful," Kristy said.

"When do you start?" Rosie asked.

"Tomorrow! Now, what's your news?"

Rosie launched into a retelling of their experience that afternoon with Zach.

"Whoa, wait a minute. This sounds like Carrie's story. Why are you telling it?"

Kristy studied Carrie. "Are you feeling all right, honey? You haven't said a word since we got home, and you've hardly eaten any of your pizza."

Carrie picked at the slice of pizza in front of her. *How did I get myself into this mess?* All she could think about was the necklace and how much trouble she was going to be in. She wanted to tell her new dad how happy she was about his job, but the only thing she managed to say was, "I'm okay, just tired."

Kristy looked doubtful, but just then the phone rang, and she got up to answer it. Carrie cringed as Kristy said, "No, Mom, I didn't see anything. Hold on, let me ask the girls."

Kristy put her hand over the mouthpiece and spoke to Rosie and Carrie. "Grandma misplaced something she bought this morning and wondered if either of you had seen it. It was in a bright red plastic bag, and she thought she left it in her room."

Rosie shook her head. "No, I didn't see anything. Did you, Carrie?"

"Uh, no, me neither," Carrie mumbled.

"No, Mom, neither of the girls saw it. Did you check with June Bug? Maybe she stole it and hid it somewhere." Kristy laughed. "Okay, see you tomorrow."

Carrie pushed her plate away and got up from the table. "I'm going to get ready for bed."

Eric and Kristy watched her climb the stairs. Eric turned to Rosie. "Are you sure she's okay? Did she hit her head when she fell off the horse?"

"No, I don't think so. She didn't fall far. Zach was almost laying down by the time she jumped off, but boy, she sure was wet and muddy!"

"Maybe it was just too much excitement," Eric decided.

"You go get ready for bed too," Kristy said. "I'll be up soon."

Upstairs, Rosie poked her head into Carrie's room and saw her lying on the bed. "It's still early. Do you want to work on the book? I was thinking what happened today would make a great chapter. I wish I'd had a camera. I don't know how I'm going to be able to draw you and Zach in the water."

The girls were working together on a horse book they planned to sell. Carrie was the author and Rosie the illustrator. They hoped to make enough money to build an indoor riding arena for their grandmother. Normally Carrie would have jumped at the chance to work on it, but she just looked up and shook her head.

"No, not tonight. I'm really tired. Night, Rosie."

Rosie stared at her for a while, disappointed, then returned to her own room.

Alone, Carrie stared at a spot on the ceiling where the roof had leaked. *I wish I had never seen that necklace! God, how can I get out of this mess?* She got up and slowly pulled a pair of pajamas out of her drawer. *At least Grandma didn't find it. God, don't let her do the laundry tonight. Tomorrow when I get there, I'll put it back and no one will ever know.*

Carrie flipped off the light and climbed back into bed. She tossed and turned, and tears filled her eyes. Unable to sleep, she got up, switched the light back on, and pulled her diary out of the desk. "I did something really bad today," she wrote. "I hope no one finds out. I don't think anyone will want to adopt a girl who steals things."

She put the pen down and stuck the diary under her bed. The tears flowed freely as she buried her face in the pillow and tried to sleep.

Downstairs, the phone rang again. "Mom? Is something wrong? You found it? Well, that's good."

The expression on Kristy's face suddenly changed. "Oh." She paused. "Okay, we'll talk to her. Bye."

"What was that all about?" Eric asked.

"It turns out the missing package was a gift for Carrie—a necklace," Kristy explained. "Mom said she found it."

Eric looked confused. "Isn't that good news?"

"When she started to do the laundry, she found it in the pocket of Carrie's jeans," Kristy said sadly.

54

"Oh—I guess that explains her behavior tonight." He paused. "Should we go talk to her?"

"Let's give her a chance to confess. Maybe if we wait until morning, she'll be ready to do that."

"Okay. I have to be at the new job early, but I'll talk to her tomorrow night."

Early the next morning, Kristy quietly entered Carrie's room and sat on the edge of her bed. "I came in to say good night last night, but you were already asleep. You must have really been tired. Did you sleep well?"

Carrie hesitated. "Not really."

"Oh? Is something wrong?"

"I don't know. I just kept waking up," Carrie said with her head down, avoiding eye contact.

Kristy waited. She hadn't slept well either, and she still wasn't sure how she should handle the situation.

"Grandma found the necklace," she said gently.

Carrie gulped. "She did?"

"Yes, when she went to do the laundry last night, she found it in your pocket. Do you want to tell me about it?"

Carrie burst into tears. "I'm sorry. I know I shouldn't have taken it. I was going to put it back today."

"Why did you lie about it last night? You said you hadn't seen it."

Carrie slowly turned over and felt around under the bed until her hand located the diary. She pulled it out and opened it to the entry she had written the night before. She held the book out.

As Kristy read, tears came to her own eyes. She handed the diary back. "Oh, Carrie." She closed her eyes and was quiet for a moment.

Her silence seemed to confirm Carrie's worst fears. She raised her head and peeked at Kristy, who finally began to speak.

"You know, I've been thinking. Maybe we should sell Zach and get you a good horse."

Carrie stopped crying and looked up, horrified. "What? You can't sell Zach. He's my very first horse and I love him."

"He's been pretty bad lately. He's spooky, hard to catch, and yesterday he laid down in the water with you. Are you sure you don't want to get rid of him?"

"I still love him, even if he has done some bad things. Can't you give him another chance?" Carrie begged.

Kristy smiled. "Carrie, that's exactly how Eric and I feel about you. Yes, you did something wrong, and then you lied about it, making it even worse, but we still love you and can't imagine not adopting you. You're already so much a part of our family."

Kristy kissed Carrie's head, and Carrie relaxed for the first time since seeing the necklace.

"Eric and I always wanted a large family, but we were never able to have any more children after Rosie. A few years ago we went through the foster parent and adoption classes, but no children were available. When Rosie told us about you, we began to feel you might be the child God had in mind for us. Over the past two years we've become certain of that. I believe God brought you to us. I don't ever want you to doubt our love for you. As much as you love Zach, we love you even more."

Carrie couldn't say anything. She cried even more, but this time they were happy tears. When she felt like she could speak again, she asked, "Is Grandma mad at me?"

"I'm sure she feels the same way about you as we do. She bought that necklace for you, Carrie. It was going to be a gift for your adoption day."

"Oh no!" Carrie fell backwards onto the bed with a loud sigh. "I messed up everything."

"If you apologize, I'm sure she'll understand." Kristy gave Carrie a long hug. "Now, why don't you go wake up your sleepy-headed soon-to-be sister? I need to get you two over to Grandma's."

Chapter 6

Forgiven

Rosie fidgeted, set her book down, and walked around Grandma's living room. "I want to go ride."

"I'm almost finished," Carrie said as she turned the page to work on the last of her math problems.

Rosie plopped back down and reluctantly opened her book again. She tipped the recliner back, and her eyes drifted upward. "Oh no!"

"What? What are you looking at?" Carrie twisted around and looked up. "June Bug, what are you doing up there? You naughty girl!" The cat was perched on one of the wide beams that ran from the loft across the living room—right over Carrie's head.

"Look, she's licking her paw and washing her face," Rosie laughed. "She wants to be nice and clean when she jumps down on your head and attacks you."

The girls laughed so loudly that Grandma stepped around the corner of the kitchen to investigate. "I don't remember math ever being that amusing." She glanced up at June Bug, then back at Carrie. "You know, she has jumped from there before."

Carrie abruptly stopped laughing. "She has?" She gathered her books, keeping an eye on June Bug, and moved out of the cat's range just in case.

"We'll be done in fifteen minutes, Grandma," Rosie promised.

Soon Rosie and Carrie were racing out the back door to let Tick out of her pen. The puppy, delighted to be free, nipped at their heels as they ran toward the barn. Carrie stopped and waited while Rosie opened the gate. She knelt down and petted the pup. "Calm down, little girl."

Tick snatched a mouthful of her hair. "Oww!" Carrie pulled her hair out of the puppy's mouth. "Don't do that," she scolded. Tick dropped to the ground remorsefully for a few seconds, then took off like a rocket to greet Jemimah, the barn cat. The puppy's enthusiasm sent Jemimah scrambling up a fencepost where she could watch from a safe distance.

Rosie patted the cat. "Don't worry, Jemimah. I don't think she'll always be this crazy."

"I hope not!" Carrie said.

As the girls neared the barn, they met Tick prancing out the front door, head high, carrying something in her mouth. "What does she have now?" Carrie asked. "She was right here just a minute ago!"

"It's one of the horse brushes. How did she get that?" The girls chased her down and got the brush away from her.

"You take the wheelbarrow first," Rosie said. "I'll try to wear her out while you're cleaning."

Carrie pushed the wheelbarrow to Zach's stall. "How are you today, Mr. Zacchaeus?" she asked cheerfully. She opened the stall door partway and let him sniff her hand, the wheelbarrow, and the pitch fork. "See, I won't hurt you."

Zach returned to the corner of the stall where he had been tracking down every scrap of leftover hay from his breakfast. Carrie was amazed at how he could wiggle his upper lip and pick up the smallest wisp of hay without getting any of the shavings. "You're a clean-plater aren't you?" She picked up the pitchfork and began cleaning.

Grandma entered the barn. "Oh no!" She smacked herself on the forehead with the palm of her hand. "I forgot the cat food again! Rosie, while you're waiting on the wheelbarrow, would you mind running back to the house and getting it for me? I bought a new bag, but I keep forgetting to bring it over."

"Come on, Tick. Let's go!" Rosie ran toward the house with Tick at her heels.

Grandma walked over to Zach's stall. "I didn't want to say anything in front of Rosie, but I want you to know that I forgive you, Carrie."

Carrie stepped into the barn aisle. Leaning on the pitchfork, she stared at the tips of her boots. "Grandma, I'm sorry. I never should have taken the necklace. It was so beautiful I felt like I had to have it, but later I felt so guilty it made me feel sick."

Grandma put her hand under Carrie's chin, tipped her head up, and looked into her eyes. "I think you've punished yourself enough. I believe in forgiving and forgetting." She gave Carrie a hug. "How is Zach today?"

"Much better. I think he's getting used to me." Carrie hugged the pony and finished cleaning his stall.

Rosie ran into the barn, out of breath, lugging a large bag of cat food. Katy and Jemimah appeared, meowing loudly, but they scattered when they saw Tick. "Set that down. I'll feed them in a minute," Grandma said as she pushed the wheelbarrow into Scamper's stall. She walked back toward Kezzie to check her water bucket.

"Are you going to ride today, Grandma?" Carrie asked.

"No, I want to watch you two work the horses in the arena. I'd like to see how well you do cantering…"

"Scamper!" Rosie yelled. "Get out of there!"

"What's he doing?" Grandma asked.

"He's in the wheelbarrow! Make him get out."

"What?" Grandma whirled around and ran toward Scamper's stall. The pony had both front legs in the wheelbarrow and looked quite pleased with himself. "What are you doing in there, you nut?" She grabbed his halter. "Get out, Rosie, in case this thing doesn't hold him much longer." Rosie slipped through the door behind Grandma and stood with Carrie outside the stall.

"All right, you silly boy, back up." Grandma pulled on Scamper's halter, but he didn't budge.

"We could let the air out of the tires," Rosie suggested.

"Now listen here." Grandma tried to reason with the pony. "I paid a lot of money for this wheelbarrow, and I don't need you to break it. It wasn't made for carrying horses."

She gave another strong tug on the halter and Scamper finally backed up, lifting first one leg, then the other out of the wheelbarrow.

"I can't believe that held him," Grandma marveled. "Too bad we didn't have a camera; that would have made a great wheelbarrow commercial!"

"I'll keep the wheelbarrow outside his stall while I'm cleaning," Rosie said.

"Good idea," Grandma agreed. "Seems like not a day goes by that these animals don't do something crazy."

When the chores were done and the horses saddled, Grandma followed the girls to the riding arena. She clipped a leash on Tick to keep her close by while the girls rode. Either the puppy knew it was for her own good or she was worn out after her romp with Rosie. She lay down contentedly at Grandma's feet. After Rosie and Carrie warmed the horses up at a walk and jog, Grandma called to Carrie, "Let's see you canter to the left."

She watched Carrie signal Zach for the canter. He responded immediately. After several laps, she stopped in front of Grandma. "Did I do it right?"

"Yes, you looked great. Can you tell which lead[2] he's on?"

"Usually," Carrie replied. "Since Kezzie doesn't like to canter, I haven't done it much, but now I love it! Aunt Julie helped me see the lead from the ground while she rode and then taught me how to feel it while I'm riding."

"Okay, work him the other direction now." Grandma leaned down to pet Tick. "Why, you little rascal. No wonder you've been so quiet." She pulled the leash out of the puppy's mouth and held it up. "You've nearly chewed

---

[2] When a horse canters, his feet move in the following sequence: outside hind, the inside hind and outside front pair, then the inside front. The extended motion of the inside front leg provides balance when the horse is turning. This is the leg that most obviously shows the horse's lead.

this all the way through! It's been so long, I've forgotten what it's like to have a puppy. I'll have to get a bone for you to chew on."

After the girls finished riding, Grandma helped them unsaddle. "You and Zach are doing very well. Do you feel comfortable about taking him on the trail ride?" Grandma asked.

"Do we have to cross any creeks?" Carrie asked.

"There's only one crossing, and we'll make sure we keep you between two of us so Zach doesn't have a chance to slow down. I'm sure he'll be fine."

"I hope so," Carrie said. "I like to swim, but I'd rather do it in a swimming pool."

"Let's see," Grandma said, thinking over the next few days. "Tomorrow Julie is dropping Elektra off here for Kristy to use on the trail ride. Then Sunday afternoon I have to pick up Lisa and Lauren at the airport. Monday is the adoption hearing and party here, and Tuesday is our trail ride." Grandma sighed. "I'm getting too old for this."

"Aww, no you're not, Grandma," Rosie insisted. "Is she, Carrie?"

Carrie didn't respond. She leaned against Zach's shoulder, thinking back over the last two years. So much had changed in her life. She had become a Christian. Her best friend was soon to become her sister. She would have a mother and father and a new last name. Although she loved her foster parents, it wasn't the same as having a family of her very own. She had her own horse now, and although she had called Grandma "Grandma" almost from the day she had first met her, in a few days she really would be her grandmother.

Rosie and Grandma watched Carrie. "Are you okay?" Rosie asked.

"Oh!" Carrie stood straight up. "I'm fine. I guess I was daydreaming."

"I wish I was being adopted," Rosie said. "This is going to be way more exciting than a birthday party."

Chapter 7

The Adoption

Carrie pulled the sheet up around her, not quite ready to wake up. She blinked an eye open and jumped when she saw two large eyes staring back at her. "What are you doing?"

Rosie was on her knees on the floor, her chin resting on top of her crossed arms on the edge of the bed just inches from Carrie's face. "I was waiting for you to wake up."

She hopped up and wandered around the room. "Mom said I couldn't wake you up, but I thought if I stared at you hard enough, you would wake up. And it worked!"

Carrie was used to Rosie's long ramblings. While Rosie talked, it gave her time to think about what she wanted to say. She waited for her to finish.

"Aren't you excited? It's your Adoption Day! I was so excited I could hardly sleep last night. I'm going to have a real sister!"

"I'm kind of nervous. I want the hearing part to be over." Carrie rolled over and propped her head up with her hand. "We'll still be best friends won't we? I mean, even when we're sisters?"

"Of course! You'll always be my best friend. Now, get out of that bed! We need to get ready."

Kristy came into Carrie's room to gather laundry. "I thought I told you not to wake her up."

"I didn't. She woke up all by herself."

Kristy rolled her eyes. "Yeah, I'll bet. You need to calm down. Our meeting isn't until after lunch. I don't know why you're up so early. You don't have to do any schoolwork today. Why don't you go ride bikes and use up some of that energy? Or you could help me with laundry."

"Laundry or a bike ride?" Rosie pondered. "That is such a hard choice, Mom." She grabbed Carrie's arm and pulled her out of bed. "Come on. Let's go, before she puts us to work."

It was quiet in their subdivision with most of the children back in school. Compared to their grandmother's place, their home was small, with a tiny backyard, but the girls' imaginations kept them entertained. That morning they were Pony Express riders. Their bikes became horses, and the play fort in the backyard was the relay station where the mail was passed from one rider to the next.

After lunch, Kristy asked them to get cleaned up and ready to go. Carrie hesitated. "I've never been in a courthouse before. Do I need to get dressed up?"

Kristy smiled. "I know it would be torture for either of you to wear a dress, so I won't ask for that, but find something nicer than your riding jeans, okay?"

The girls rushed off. Sounds of dresser drawers and closet doors opening and closing and water running drifted down the stairs. Fifteen minutes later, they returned to the kitchen, scrubbed clean and wearing their best Sunday dresses.

"What do you think?" Rosie beamed.

"Look at you two! I can't believe it."

"It's such an important day, we agreed it was worth wearing dresses," Rosie explained.

"But—" Carrie smiled and pulled a backpack from behind her back, "we packed our jeans in here, to change into as soon as we get to Grandma's house."

"You girls are too much. Let's get going. Your dad's meeting us at the courthouse."

They parked in front of the large county courthouse and walked up a long flight of brick steps. Eric met them inside the front door. "Is everyone ready?"

Carrie and Rosie nodded, nervousness suddenly overriding their excitement.

"The room is this way." Their footsteps echoed as the girls followed Eric down a long hallway with tall ceilings. They entered a conference room with a huge polished wood table. Rosie and Carrie looked small sitting beside Kristy and Eric.

"This doesn't look like a courtroom," Carrie whispered to Rosie. She smiled at Judy and Ross Robinson, seated across the table from her. She recognized her social worker, but not the two men.

"I think everyone is here," the man at the end of the long table said in a deep, booming voice. He looked back and forth between the girls. "Which one of you is Carrie?"

Carrie slowly raised her hand. "I am." Her voice quivered a bit as she spoke.

"I thought so. It's nice to meet you, Carrie. I'm Judge Thomas. I'm glad I could be part of this special day." He smiled at her and passed some papers to the attorney. "I believe all the paperwork is in order."

The girls watched Kristy and Eric look over the papers and discuss legal details. Rosie's legs couldn't quite reach the floor when she sat back in her chair. She swung her legs back and forth and looked around the room. Carrie watched the judge nervously. Rosie caught Carrie's attention and signed something to her.

Carrie frowned and shrugged her shoulders. "What?" she mouthed silently.

Rosie repeated her message. Carrie still didn't understand and turned her attention back to the adults' conversation.

After twenty minutes, the judge looked at Carrie. "Young lady, you are now legally, Carrie Jackson. You're part of a special family. I've known your grandmother for a long time—very good woman."

Carrie blinked. "It's over? I didn't even have to do anything?"

"In Ohio, children don't have to consent to an adoption unless they're over twelve, so I didn't ask you," the judge explained. Sensing Carrie's disappointment, he quickly added. "Do you want to be adopted?"

"Yes, I do," Carrie replied solemnly, as if she had been practicing her answer.

"Well, then, it's official." He walked over and shook Carrie's hand. "Congratulations."

"Thank you," Carrie said with a big smile.

"I want to get a picture of all of you with the judge," Judy said.

"Oh, thanks. I didn't think about that." Kristy gathered the girls and Eric around her.

After several photos, they began to leave the courthouse. Kristy waved to the Robinsons as they turned toward their car. "You're coming to the party aren't you?"

"We wouldn't miss it," Judy replied.

Carrie and Rosie piled into the backseat of the car. Rosie nudged Carrie. "Scoot over, sis!"

Carrie grinned. "I can't believe I have a real sister."

"Oh, no. Don't start that again," Rosie moaned.

"What were you signing to me during the adoption?" Carrie asked.

"Oh yeah," Rosie laughed. "I was saying I can't wait until you open the present I got you."

When they arrived at Grandma's, there were so many cars they couldn't pull in the driveway.

Carrie stared. "Who are all these people?"

"I imagine they're all people who want to wish you a happy adoption day!" Eric replied.

The first thing Carrie saw inside the house was a large banner with "Carrie Jackson" in large, colorful letters. There were balloons and streamers and more people than Carrie could count. She had never had so many hugs and good wishes in her entire life. All she could do was smile and say "Thank you" over and over again.

After several hours, people gradually began to leave until only family was left. Lisa smiled at Carrie, who looked a little dazed. "Are you feeling overwhelmed?"

"Yeah."

"Why don't you have a seat? I think there are a few presents for you." Lisa guided Carrie toward the couch.

Rosie and Carrie sat side by side, and the cousins gathered around. "You can open mine first." Rosie eagerly handed Carrie her gift.

Carrie unwrapped the box and pulled out a wooden plaque with *Zach* carved into it.

"It's for Zach's stall," Rosie explained. "I made it myself. Well, Dad helped a little."

"I love it!"

Jessie and Jamie handed Carrie their gift next. Carrie unwrapped it to find two western shirts, exactly alike. She held them up with a puzzled look.

"One's for you and one's for Rosie," Jessie explained. "We heard you two wanted to be twins, like us, so we thought this would help."

"Oh." Carrie smiled and handed one of the shirts to Rosie. "I can't wait to try it on. Green is my favorite color!" Carrie said.

"I wish we lived closer so I could see you more often," Lauren said. "Rosie told me you like to write. I do too. I thought this might help us get to know each other better." She held her gift out.

Carrie carefully unwrapped it. "Oh, it's beautiful," she said, holding up stationery with a band of wild Mustangs across the top. "Maybe you could help with the book Rosie and I are working on. I'm writing it, and Rosie is drawing the pictures."

"That sounds like fun," Lauren agreed.

When Carrie had opened the last gift, she thanked everyone again, and Eric stood up. He started to speak, then for a moment looked like he might cry. Wiping his eyes, he mumbled something about his allergies being bad this time of year and turned to face Carrie. "You've received a lot of nice gifts today, but Kristy and I received the best gift of all: another daughter to love and care for. I'm so thankful that God brought you into our lives." He gave Carrie a hug. "Why don't we all join together in prayer?"

Everyone formed a circle and held hands. Eric led them in prayer and asked God to bless their lives together.

"That," Lisa said as the circle broke up, "was the perfect ending to a perfect day."

The girls were exhausted when they climbed into the car for the trip home. Carrie's mind ran back over the events of the day—the kind things people had said to her and the many gifts she had received. With a twinge of disappointment, she thought about the necklace. She knew she didn't deserve it, but she had secretly hoped Grandma might give it to her anyway.

"You girls get ready for bed," Kristy said after they had taken Carrie's gifts up to her room. "We need to be up and over to Mom's early in the morning. In case you've forgotten, we have a trail ride tomorrow."

When they came back to Carrie's room to kiss her good night, Kristy and Eric were greeted with giggles as two heads popped out from under the covers.

"You can stay in here tonight, Rosie, if you promise to get to sleep soon," Kristy said. She and Eric kissed both the girls.

"I'm practically asleep already," Rosie assured her. "Good night, Mom. Good night, Dad. Good night, sister."

Carrie hesitated a moment. She couldn't remember ever calling anyone "Mom" or "Dad" before. "Good night,

Mom and Dad." It felt a little strange, but she liked the sound of it.

Chapter 8
The Trail Ride

"Carrie, we're sorry we have to miss the trail ride," Lisa said. She finished packing her remaining things into a bag. "My mother-in-law is having surgery this morning, and I promised to stay with her at the hospital. Then we catch a plane back to Texas tonight. I was only able to get a couple days off work."

"That's okay. Thank you for coming," Carrie said shyly.

"Oh, you're welcome. It was a wonderful party," Lisa said, smiling at her new niece.

"I think I'm going to leave these up for a while," Grandma said, pointing to Carrie's banner and decorations. "They remind me of what a wonderful new granddaughter I have."

"Don't forget to write," Lauren reminded Carrie.

"I'll write my first letter tonight and tell you about the trail ride," Carrie said.

"We need to be going, and you have horses to get ready." Lisa started for the door. "Be careful, everyone."

Grandma, Kristy, and the girls stood on the porch watching and waving until Lisa's car was out of sight.

"All right, who's ready for a trail ride?" Grandma asked.

"Let's go!" Carrie and Rosie shouted.

Soon they were busy loading tack and equipment into the horse trailer.

"That's it," Rosie declared.

"Are you sure?" Grandma asked. "Make sure there's a saddle, blanket, and bridle for each horse. "And a girth on each of the saddles. Once, we ended up at the trail with Julie's saddle, but no girth. She rode bareback that day. I don't want anything like that happening today."

Kristy helped the girls check over everything again. "Yep, we're good, Mom."

"Okay, we're ready for the horses then," Grandma said. "Let's put Zach and Scamper in first and Kezzie and Elektra in the back."

After the horses were loaded, everyone climbed into the truck and they started on their way. Grandma glanced at her watch. "It's only eight o'clock. I can't believe we're actually leaving on time. That should put us at the trails around nine-thirty and ready to ride by ten."

"Sounds good to me," Kristy said.

"What are we doing for lunch?" Rosie asked.

"We packed lunches to eat on the trail," Grandma replied.

"I'm hungry already," Carrie said.

"Let's work on sign language," Rosie suggested. "If you learn more of it, we can use it like a secret code." Rosie showed Carrie how to spell her name, taught her a few new signs, and then began to quiz her on them.

"Church," Rosie said.

Carrie slowly made a C-shape with her fingers and moved it in a circular motion over her other hand.

Rosie laughed loudly. "No, that means chocolate."

Carrie sighed with frustration. "I just can't remember them."

"You'll learn," Kristy encouraged. "Rosie's had a lot more practice than you. You almost had it. Just make that C-shape again and, instead of circling with it, tap the back of your other hand twice."

Rosie watched as Carrie tried again. "That's it! Just remember you stir chocolate, but you don't stir church."

When the girls tired of signing, they sang songs and played games until they pulled into the park entrance. "Here we are," Grandma announced. The horseman's camp was deserted, so she parked near the restrooms and water faucet.

Kristy looked around. "It looks like we have the park to ourselves today. It's so quiet."

"That might be good," Grandma said. "No horses to distract Zach his first time out."

Soon they had all four horses saddled, bridled, and ready to start on the trail. "Do you need a map, Mom?" Kristy asked.

"Not really. Kezzie and I have ridden here so many times we have the trails memorized... but go ahead and pick up a couple for Carrie and Rosie."

Kristy walked over to the information board, but came back empty-handed. "There weren't any there." She frowned.

"No problem. We'll be fine," Grandma said.

Rosie ran back to the truck and returned, trying to pull her favorite red sweatshirt over her helmeted head. The shirt covered her face, but wouldn't stretch enough to slide down over the helmet. She held her arms out and stumbled toward the others.

Kristy stared at her and shook her head. "Rosie, take your helmet off. You're going to ruin that shirt by stretching it like that. Aren't you going to be hot with that on, anyway?"

"I'm cold." Rosie pulled the sweatshirt off, removed her helmet and slipped the shirt back over her head. The weather had been typical for early fall in Ohio. Mornings were crisp and cool, later warming to sunny afternoons with incredible blue skies.

Rosie strapped her helmet on and climbed on Scamper. "I'll tie it to my saddle when I get too warm."

The others mounted their horses. Carrie patted Zach's neck. "Okay, boy. This is your first real trail ride. You better behave." She rode over beside Rosie.

Grandma pointed across the road. "Let's take that trail. It's a good place to start."

Grandma and Kezzie led the group, followed by Rosie, Carrie, and Kristy. Almost immediately the trail sloped downward, leading to the bottom of a steep ravine. The horses carefully picked their way down the path.

When they reached the bottom, Grandma twisted in her saddle to check on the girls. "How are you doing back there?"

"Good," Carrie replied. "I think Zach likes trail riding."

Although most of the trail was dry, the ground at the bottom of the ravine was muddy and rutted with the tracks of horses that had passed through before.

"Be careful Zach doesn't give you a mud bath," Rosie laughed.

"I don't think he likes to lay down in the mud," Carrie replied.

"Scamper, watch out!" Rosie yelled. She jerked the reins, stood in her left stirrup and pulled her right leg up over Scamper's hindquarters. "You almost took my knee off," Rosie scolded. In trying to avoid the mud, Scamper had moved far to the right and brushed up against a tree at the side of the trail. Rosie sat back down and concentrated on keeping Scamper in the center of the path.

They climbed up the other side of the ravine and entered a wooded area. "This is all state forest here," Grandma explained to the girls. "We'll have to come back in a few more weeks, when the trees are in full color."

Kezzie led the way along the narrow dirt trail, avoiding tree roots and stumps and calmly walking over downed logs. They were surrounded by trees clothed with bright green leaves that would soon be changing color and falling to the ground. Suddenly, Kezzie came to a dead stop. Scamper wasn't paying close attention and ran into the back of her. She flattened her ears and gave him a warning look, then raised her head high and looked off to the right.

"What are you stopping for, Grandma?" Rosie asked.

"I don't know. Kezzie stopped on her own. She must see something." Grandma looked through the trees, straining to see what it was that had captured her horse's attention.

Kristy caught up with them. "I see it."

"See what?" Grandma asked.

"I'm not sure, but I think it's a flock of wild turkeys." Kristy pointed through the trees to a small clearing in the distance. "They're really far away, but I see something bobbing up and down."

"Oh, I see them," Rosie said excitedly.

"Me too," added Carrie.

"Well, I'm going to trust you all. I guess these eyes are too old to see wild turkeys a mile away." Grandma patted Kezzie's neck. "That's nice of you to warn us about them,

"Talk to me, Mom," Kristy pleaded. She looked her over, trying to determine the extent of her injuries. Grandma lay on her back, her clothes stained with dirt and mud. A long scrape stretched across her cheek. Kristy gently wiped the blood from her mother's face with her shirt sleeve. She was relieved to see that the wound didn't look serious; however she caught her breath when she noticed blood seeping through the shirt sleeve of Grandma's right arm. Her right leg was bent at a peculiar angle.

Kristy felt sick to her stomach and thought she might faint. She sat down and closed her eyes. *God, Lisa's the nurse. I don't know how to handle this. I need Your help.* She took a deep breath and released it slowly.

"I 'm… o-k-ay."

She opened her eyes and saw her mother looking up at her.

"Oh, Mom, you're not okay." Kristy wiped the tears from her eyes so she could see more clearly. Grandma tried to raise herself up and winced in pain as the motion jostled her leg.

"H-o-w is Kezzie?" Grandma asked and lay back down.

Kristy looked up the hill toward Rosie and Carrie. "Go check on Kezzie. Be careful. It's really steep."

Glad to have something to do, Rosie and Carrie cautiously started down the hill. They soon discovered that the easiest way was to sit and scoot down the steep slope.

They went on past Kristy and Grandma, down to where Kezzie was lying quietly.

"You're going to be okay, girl," Carrie said, gently stroking Kezzie's neck. She bent down and removed the horse's bridle, attaching a lead rope to her halter.

"Stand back if she tries to get up, in case she falls again," Kristy called down to them.

Carrie looked at the horse more closely. "That's weird," she said as she ran her hand over the horse's neck again. "What are these?" She pointed to several large welts. "Look, she has them all over."

"Strange," Rosie replied. "Mom will know."

Kezzie raised her head and straightened her front legs.

"Look out! She's trying to stand up," Rosie said. She and Carrie jumped back out of the horse's way. Kezzie struggled, but finally got to her feet, holding one of her legs up off the ground. She nuzzled Carrie.

"Aww, she's asking me for help." Carrie kissed her on the forehead, one of the few places on her body not covered in welts. "What can we do for her?"

"Let's get her saddle off." Rosie held the lead rope while Carrie unfastened the girth and removed the saddle. It was scraped and dirty, but still in one piece.

Carrie patted Kezzie. "Does that make you feel better?" She walked over and set the saddle down at the base of a tree.

"Oh no!" Rosie said. "Look, her leg is bleeding."

Carrie returned and looked at Kezzie's leg. A cut stretched across the front of her right, front cannon bone. "You poor girl."

"Hold onto her. I'm going to get my water bottle and rinse the dirt off that cut." Rosie started toward the trail where she had left Scamper tied.

Kristy looked down the hill and saw that the horse was standing. "Kezzie's up, Mom. I think she's okay."

"Thank You," Grandma whispered. Kristy knew she wasn't speaking to her.

Grandma turned to Kristy. "Take this off."

"What do you mean? Your helmet?"

Grandma nodded.

"I don't know." Kristy shook her head. "We shouldn't do that. You might have a neck injury."

Grandma raised her head off the ground and twisted it to the left and right. "It's fine."

"If you're sure," Kristy said reluctantly. She loosened the nylon straps. As she gently lifted Grandma's head just far enough off the ground to remove the helmet, she noticed a large crack on its left side.

Grandma laid her head back on the ground. "That's better."

"It's a good thing you had this on." Kristy held up the damaged helmet.

"I think she rolled over me and clipped me in the head with one of her hooves. It happened so fast."

"Don't talk so much, Mom. You need to lie still. I don't know what happened, but it must have been awful for Kezzie to freak out like that."

Grandma moaned as she tried to find a comfortable position.

Chapter 9

The Rescue

Kristy carefully peeled back Grandma's sleeve far enough to see the wound that ran the length of her forearm. Her face twisted into a grimace. She knew she had to stop the bleeding.

"Girls, come up here. Hurry! Kezzie won't go anywhere."

Rosie and Carrie scrambled back up the hill. Grandma smiled weakly when she saw them.

"Rosie, do you still have your sweatshirt?"

Rosie ran back to get the shirt that she had tied to the back of her saddle and handed it to her mother.

Kristy held the body of the shirt and extended the sleeve to Rosie. "Here, pull on this."

Rosie pulled. The shirt stretched, but held together. "What are you doing, Mom?"

"Grandma's arm has a nasty gash. I'm trying to tear this so I can make a bandage to stop the bleeding."

Rosie fished around in the pocket of her jeans and pulled out a small knife. "Here."

Kristy grabbed the knife, opened the blade, and poked a hole in the shirt where the sleeve joined the shoulder. She ripped the sleeve off and handed it to Carrie. From the remainder of the shirt, she cut out a section to make a square bandage, which she held firmly over the wound on Grandma's arm.

"I'm trying to decide the best way to get help," Kristy said, keeping pressure on the wound. "We've ridden about two hours from the campground."

Rosie looked around. "Do you think there's a road somewhere?"

"Maybe, but if I leave the trail and get lost it will take even longer to find help. I wish I had a map." Kristy glanced over at her mother. "Mom?" she said softly. Grandma turned to look at her.

Kristy leaned down. "Do you know if there's a road around here?"

Grandma looked puzzled and closed her eyes. "I don't remember," she said faintly.

"That's okay, Mom. There's a good chance I'd get lost anyway if I got off the trail."

"Carrie and I could ride back for help, and you could stay with Grandma," Rosie offered.

Carrie nodded eagerly.

"I thought about that, but there was no one at the campground—I'll probably have to drive somewhere to get help." Kristy pulled her phone out of her pocket and tossed it to Rosie. "See if you can get a signal."

Rosie held the phone up and walked around. "No, nothing," she said, frowning.

Kristy released the pressure on Grandma's arm and looked at the bandage. It was nearly soaked through, but the bleeding seemed to have stopped. "Carrie, hand me that sleeve." Kristy carefully wound the sleeve around Grandma's arm, over the top of the bandage. "I need something to tie this with."

Rosie ran to Kezzie's saddle and cut off one of the long leather ties. She hurried back and handed it to her mother. Kristy tied the sleeve snugly in place around Grandma's arm. "There; that should do for now. Mom, don't move that arm or it might start bleeding again."

Kristy turned to the girls. "There's no way we can move her. Her leg is definitely broken, and I don't want her arm to bleed anymore."

The girls grew pale as they noticed the unnatural bend in Grandma's leg.

"I think the best option is for me to ride back along the same trail. I can probably make it in about an hour." Kristy stood up and looked over the horses. "I'm counting on you two to take care of Grandma and Kezzie. Don't let either of them move. If, by any chance, other riders come by, send them off for help too. Someone familiar with the trails might know of a quicker way out of here."

"Mom, take Scamper," Rosie urged. "He's good on the trails, and he doesn't mind going by himself."

"Good idea!"

"Oh," Carrie said, "Kezzie has a cut on her leg and big bumps all over her."

"You two get Scamper ready for me, and I'll check her real quick."

Rosie and Carrie ran to get Scamper. They lengthened the stirrups as far as they would go and put the reins up over the saddle horn. One look at Kezzie was all it took for Kristy to realize what had happened. "You poor girl, we're going to get you out of here." She patted Kezzie's forehead and hurried back to the trail.

"Don't go near the top of that hill!" Kristy yelled at the girls as she ran toward Scamper.

"Why not?" Rosie asked, alarmed by the tone of her mother's voice.

Kristy grabbed the reins and jumped into the saddle. "From the looks of Kezzie, I'd say she stirred up a huge hornets' nest up there. Poor thing, she probably has a hundred stings."

Carrie and Rosie stared at each other, wide-eyed.

"Talk to Grandma—keep her awake," Kristy said. "And keep praying. I'll get back with help as soon as I can." She dug her heels into Scamper's sides, and he leaped into a canter.

"Hurry, Mom!"

Rosie and Carrie stood and watched until they disappeared down the trail; the weight of responsibility settling heavily onto their small shoulders.

(from photo)

Rosie slowly turned around. "Let's move the horses off the hill." The girls led Zach and Elektra down to a small clearing, not far from Kezzie. They removed the lead ropes that were attached to the saddles and fastened them to the halters the horses wore under their bridles. They pulled the bridles off and hung them over the saddle horns.

Kezzie looked their way and nickered. She tried to move toward them. "No!" Carrie yelled. "Don't move, Kezzie." She ran to grab her lead rope.

"You stay with Kezzie and I'll stay with Grandma." Rosie ran over to Kezzie's saddle and pulled a water bottle out of the saddlebag. "She might be thirsty." She hurried back up to Grandma's side.

"Mom went to get help." She knelt down beside her. "Are you thirsty?"

Grandma nodded. Rosie tried to pour the water into her mouth, but most of it ended up on the ground.

"Did you get any of that?"

Grandma nodded again and squeezed Rosie's hand. Rosie couldn't remember when she had ever been this frightened. Her stomach felt like it was tied into a giant knot. "You're going to be okay, Grandma," she said, as much to convince herself as her grandmother.

The sight of her grandmother's twisted leg made her shudder. She prayed silently that her mother would be back soon with help. *Now, what did Mom say?* She tried to remember her mother's instructions. *Oh, yeah, talk to Grandma and keep her awake.* Talking was something Rosie was good at, especially when she was nervous. She began to chatter away, describing the adoption hearing from the day before, what she was studying for school, how many horse shows she and Scamper were going to win, and anything and everything else that popped into her mind. Every few minutes she would pause and say, "Are you doing okay?" Grandma would nod, and Rosie would resume the one-sided conversation.

Further down the hill, Carrie sang to Kezzie and petted her lovingly. Even though she had her own horse now, she had learned to ride on Kezzie and had won her first, and only, trophy with her. She still loved the horse dearly. Kezzie liked Rosie, but she seemed to love Carrie almost as much as she loved Grandma.

Every so often, Rosie and Carrie switched places. "What time do you think it is?" Carrie called up to Rosie. "It seems like it's been a long time."

"I don't know. I don't have a watch."

"Does Grandma?"

Rosie looked at her grandmother's right arm beside her, then moved so she could see her left. "Grandma, can I take your watch off?"

Grandma nodded and started to raise her right arm.

"No, no! Don't move that arm." Rosie was horrified, fearing that the cut on Grandma's arm would start bleeding again. "It's on the other one."

"Oh." Grandma raised her other arm. Rosie removed the watch. She wiped the mud off the face and noticed the glass was cracked. She held it up to her ear and heard it ticking.

"If this is still working, it's one o'clock," Rosie said.

"Mom thought it would take her an hour to get back to the campground," Carrie said. "Maybe someone will be here soon." They focused their attention back on Grandma and Kezzie and waited.

"One-thirty," Rosie called out. "I thought sure someone would be here by now."

"It shouldn't be too much longer," Carrie said.

"Wait! Did you hear that?"

They both stood perfectly still and listened.

"Someone's coming through the woods," Carrie said excitedly. She ran up toward Rosie. They both turned in the direction of the noise and watched. "I heard it again," she said.

"Me too. Grandma, someone's coming!"

Suddenly, the brush parted in front of them, and a head appeared in the clearing.

"Aw, it's just a deer." Rosie sighed with disappointment. The small doe seemed surprised to see the girls. The three stood motionless, staring at each other. Finally the doe decided the girls were not dangerous and turned to browse on the bushes along the trail.

Carrie returned to Kezzie, and Rosie sat back down by Grandma, who seemed to be asleep. *Oh, no, I'm supposed to keep her awake!* She leaned down and whispered, "Are you awake, Grandma?"

Grandma's eyes remained closed, but she nodded. Rosie sighed with relief. After another fifteen minutes she stood and yelled down to Carrie, "Let's trade places again." Rosie kept one eye on Grandma and waited for Carrie to make it up the hill.

"Watch her carefully—she's getting sleepy," Rosie warned. As she started down toward Kezzie, Carrie grabbed her arm.

"I heard something!" Carrie cocked her head in the direction of the sound.

"I didn't hear anything. It was probably just another deer." Rosie tried to push past her, but Carrie held her arm firmly.

"No, I really heard something. It sounded like a motorcycle."

They listened again.

"I hear it!" Rosie said excitedly.

The noise grew louder. Soon they saw a four-wheeler pop through the trees. Two men were riding and two more followed on foot.

Rosie dropped to the ground and squeezed her grandmother's shoulder. "They're here, Grandma!"

"Hi girls. Don't worry. We're going to take care of your grandmother." The men jumped off the vehicle and quickly got to work.

Rosie and Carrie backed away to give them room. The girls stood side by side and watched from a distance as the medics attached an oxygen tube and IV.

"What are they doing?" Carrie whispered.

"I don't know. Maybe they do that to everyone who's injured," Rosie replied.

When they finished caring for Grandma, one of the paramedics walked over to the girls. "Your dad will be here soon. He's bringing a veterinarian with him. Will you be okay until he arrives?"

Rosie and Carrie nodded.

"We'll get your grandmother out of here and on her way to the hospital." The men carefully lifted her onto a large board. Tears came to the girls' eyes as Grandma cried out in pain. Strapped securely, with two men on each side, she lay still as they slowly raised the board.

The leader turned to Rosie and Carrie. "We're going to carry her to the road. It will take a little longer, but with that leg, it will be easier on her. It would be too painful for her to bump around on a four-wheeler."

He looked down at Grandma, "We're not as fast as that horse of yours, but we'll get you out. Are you ready?"

Grandma smiled and nodded. "Take care of Kezzie," she said to the girls."

"Don't worry," the paramedic reassured her. "A veterinarian is on the way."

He nodded to the other men. "Let's go."

The girls watched the men carry their grandmother into the woods. When they could no longer see them, they turned and walked back toward Kezzie to wait some more.

"Grandma's on her way to the hospital," Carrie informed Kezzie as she stroked the horse's forehead. "Someone will be here soon to help you, girl." Kezzie raised her head and licked Carrie's hand.

Rosie dropped down to the ground. She picked up a stick and scratched the dirt with it, then tossed it into the brush and started to sob. "This is all my fault."

Carrie turned to look at her, bewildered. She had always thought of Rosie as stronger than herself. "What do you mean? How could it be your fault?"

"If I hadn't had the idea to go on the trail ride, Grandma and Kezzie wouldn't have gotten hurt." She snapped another stick in two and flung the pieces angrily aside.

Carrie sat down beside Rosie and put her arm around her. "If it's your fault, then it's my fault too."

"What? Why?"

"If I hadn't been adopted, then you wouldn't have had the idea for the trail ride."

Rosie was quiet for a moment. "Why did Grandma have to get hurt?" She looked around. "Where is Dad anyway? What's taking so long?"

Rosie walked over to the horses. Zach nickered as he saw her approach. He looked at her as if asking, "What are we doing here?"

"We'll get you back home soon, boy." She pressed her cheek against his neck and put her arms around him as the tears started again. "You miss your friend, Scamper, don't you?" Rosie wiped away the tears and walked over to Elektra. "How are you, girl? This isn't what you expected, is it?" She petted the horse and returned to where Carrie was still sitting.

"You okay?" Carrie asked.

"Yeah."

They sat quietly together. Occasionally one of them would get up and make the rounds, checking each of the horses. Finally they heard a welcome sound: the growl of another four-wheeler.

"That's gotta be Dad." Rosie jumped up and moved toward the area where the medics had broken through the brush.

"Dad! You're finally here."

Eric stopped the four-wheeler at a distance so he wouldn't scare the horses. Dr. Rings climbed off the back, then Eric jumped off. The girls ran to him and he wrapped them both in a strong hug.

"Are we ever glad to see you!" Rosie said.

Dr. Rings began gathering her equipment from the storage compartments. Rosie stared at her for a moment. "Dr. Rings? They said a vet was coming, but I didn't think it would be you."

"Hi girls. I turn up in the strangest places, don't I?" She smiled and hurried back to her work.

"When your mom made it to the park office, she called me at work," Eric explained. "I just happened to catch Dr. Rings in between appointments, and she followed me to the park. We made it here as quickly as we could, although it wasn't fast enough for me."

"Me either," Rosie agreed. "Where's Mom? I thought she was coming back."

"She's at the hospital. I'll explain it all later," Eric said. "Let's help Dr. Rings with Kezzie."

"Can you carry these for me?" Dr. Rings handed the girls a bandage box and a bag with emergency supplies. "I saved this horse once, and I'm sure I can save her again. They say cats have nine lives, but I believe horses have even more."

"She took care of Scamper when he was born too," Rosie said to Carrie as they followed the vet.

Dr. Rings slowly approached Kezzie. "You remember me, girl? We share the same birthday." She had been called out early in the morning the day Kezzie was born, when her mother, Satin, had rejected her. The vet let the horse smell the equipment. Kezzie snorted and jerked back, raising her head high. "Can someone hold her and keep her quiet?"

"I will." Carrie eagerly grabbed the lead rope. "Hold still, Kezzie. Dr. Rings is going to fix your leg."

Kezzie lowered her head and stood calmly while Carrie scratched behind her ears.

"You're better than a horse whisperer." Dr. Rings smiled at Carrie. "I think you have that horse hypnotized. That's just what I needed." She bent down to examine Kezzie's injured leg. Eric moved around so he could watch.

"Hmm. She's lacerated the front of that right, front leg. Probably scraped it on a sharp rock as she came down the hill."

Rosie handed Dr. Rings the bandage. The vet carefully wrapped the large, puffy, white bandage around Kezzie's leg, then wound a support wrap around it to hold the bandage in place. "The wound doesn't look too serious, but she'll need to be radiographed later to check for bone sequestra."

Rosie frowned. "What's sekestria?"

Dr. Rings smiled. "Sequestra are bone chips. A chip can break off when there's an injury involving a blow to a bone, often the cannon bone, by a kick, or in this case Kezzie crashing into a rock."

"Is that serious?" Eric asked.

"If there is a chip, it may become infected and would have to be removed surgically or the wound won't heal."

Dr. Rings examined her work. "I think that will do it. Carrie, see if you can get her to take a step."

Carrie tugged gently on the lead rope. Kezzie looked at her questioningly, afraid to move, but with a little more coaxing Carrie got her to take a step. It was more of a hop than a walk, since she couldn't put much weight on the injured leg, but she was moving.

"All right," Eric directed, "let's start for the trailer. Dr. Rings, could you lead Zach? Carrie's doing so well with Kezzie, I think she should take her. Rosie, you might as well hop on Elektra, and I'll lead you. If Carrie gets tired, you two can switch places. This is going to be slow going. We'll let Kezzie stop and rest a lot."

As they made their way through the woods, Zach and Elektra seemed to sense that Kezzie was hurt. They walked slowly and stopped often to look back and see how she was doing.

"It will be a little easier when we get to level ground," Eric said.

An hour and a half later, they arrived at the trailer. "Put Kezzie in last," Eric said. "Our first stop is going to be the veterinary hospital."

He turned to Dr. Rings. "Thanks for your help. Mom will be so happy when she finds out you took care of Kezzie."

"Glad to do it. I think she'll be okay. I'll head back and pick up the four-wheeler and return it to the park office. Is there anything else I can do?"

"Oh, Dad," Rosie said. "We left Kezzie's saddle back there."

"I'll get it," Dr. Rings offered.

"Thanks," Eric replied. "I'll connect with you tomorrow to pick it up."

The truck pulled out and the girls sank back into the comfortable seats, relaxing for the first time since the accident.

"I wonder how Grandma is," Rosie wondered.

"Don't worry—I'm sure she's getting excellent care. Your mom and Julie are there, and I wouldn't be surprised if Lisa is with them by now. We need to make sure Kezzie is taken care of so your grandmother doesn't worry about her."

Rosie's stomach growled loudly. She laughed. "My stomach is saying, 'Feed me.'"

"I'm kind of hungry too," Carrie said. "I forgot all about eating."

"We can get our lunches out of—oh, I guess not," Rosie said. "They're in Kezzie's saddlebag back on the trail."

"After we drop Kezzie off, I'll stop and get you something to eat," Eric promised. "Then we'll take Zach and Elektra home and run over to the hospital."

"Are you tired, Carrie? You know, you didn't have to lead Kezzie the whole way. You could have ridden Elektra for a while."

Carrie paused and turned to look at Rosie, trying to determine whether she was mad at her. "Yeah, I'm tired. I was more worried about Kezzie though. Every time she took a step she would look at me with her big, sad eyes. If she could keep going while she was in so much pain, I felt like I needed to stay with her."

Rosie nodded. "You did a great job, sis."

Carrie smiled. "You did too. You were great with Grandma. I couldn't keep myself from looking at her leg, then I would start to feel sick."

Eric looked at the girls. "I'm proud of you both, and I know your mom and Grandma will be too."

After the horses were all taken care of, it was nearly eight o'clock by the time they reached the hospital. Kristy met them in the waiting room.

"How is Grandma?" Rosie and Carrie asked.

"She's okay. They operated and put a pin in her leg and casted it. She has thirty stitches in her arm and lots of scrapes and bruises, but no internal injuries. They want to keep her overnight for observation, but unless some complications arise, she should be able to go home sometime tomorrow."

Rosie and Carrie looked at each other, relief spreading across both their faces.

"She's anxious to see you two and to hear how Kezzie is."

"I told the people at the veterinary hospital to do whatever is necessary for Kezzie," Eric said. "They're supposed to call me after they've examined her."

"Let's go up. She's on the fifth floor," Kristy said.

Rosie grabbed her mom's right hand, and Carrie moved to take the other as they started toward the elevator.

Chapter 10

Grandma's Surprise

The girls stepped out of the elevator and started down the corridor. The hospital was a little frightening with its strong medicinal smell, intercoms calling doctors to emergencies, and the continual beeping of equipment. Kristy led them to Grandma's room, where Lisa and Julie were sitting and talking quietly.

The girls' eyes widened when they saw their grandmother lying in the bed, pale and framed by white hospital sheets. The grandmother they knew was tanned and strong, always busy working around the house or barn.

Grandma's eyes flickered and she slowly opened one of them.

Rosie and Carrie moved closer. "You're awake! How do you feel, Grandma?"

"Not too bad."

"Oh Grandma, I'm sorry about the trail ride. It was my idea, but I didn't think you would get hurt." Rosie started crying. Carrie was fighting back tears also.

"Come here and give me a hug, you two. It was not your fault, Rosie. Don't you think that for a minute. I'm just glad it wasn't one of you that ran into that nest of hornets. And it will take a lot more than a broken leg and a few cuts and bruises to stop me."

The girls managed to smile. This sounded more like the Grandma they knew.

"Now, tell me how Kezzie's doing."

"She's at the hospital," Carrie said, "but Dr. Rings thinks she's going to be okay."

"You should have seen Carrie," Rosie said. "She led Kezzie all the way back to the trailer by herself. Kezzie was nice and quiet when Carrie stayed beside her."

"Thank you, Carrie! I knew you girls would take good care of her. I'm so glad Dr. Rings was available. That was certainly an answer to my prayers." Grandma closed her eyes again.

Rosie and Carrie turned toward Kristy with a concerned look.

"She's drowsy from the anesthetic and the pain medication," Lisa explained.

Carrie suddenly remembered Grandma's puppy. "Oh no, what about Tick?" she whispered.

"We put her in the pen when we left this morning," Kristy said. "She's safe, but I'm sure she's a very hungry puppy right now." She turned toward Eric. "Would you mind calling the Robinsons? Explain what's happened and ask Ross if he would run over and feed Tick." Eric nodded and stepped into the hallway to make a quick phone call.

"Carrie?"

Carrie turned around. "What, Grandma? I thought you were asleep again."

"I was just resting." Grandma smiled. "I had a gift I was going to give you when we stopped for lunch. It's in Kezzie's saddlebag. I think you know what it is. I really want you to have it. If you're at my house tomorrow, go ahead and get it out."

Rosie looked blankly at Grandma. "Gift? How would Carrie know what it is, if it's a gift?"

"Oh no, Grandma—we don't have Kezzie's saddle! We left it at the trail," Carrie said.

Eric stepped back into the room. "That's right. Dr. Rings was going to pick it up. I'll have to track her down tomorrow to see if she remembered it."

"Well, that gift has had quite an adventurous life, hasn't it?" Grandma winked at Carrie.

"What gift?" Rosie repeated. "I don't know what you're talking about. Is this some kind of secret or something?" She looked back and forth from Grandma to Carrie.

"Don't worry about it, Rosie," Kristy said firmly. "Carrie will tell you when she's ready."

Rosie was still curious, but the tone of her mother's voice convinced her not to pursue the matter—at least, not now. She turned to Lisa. "I thought you were going back to Texas today, Aunt Lisa. And where is Lauren?"

"Your mom did a super job of handling the emergency on the trail, but I thought she might appreciate some help with the nursing duties when Mom gets home." Lisa glanced at her watch. "Robert should be picking Lauren up at the airport about now. I hope she's okay. This is the first time she's flown alone. I'll fly back sometime next week if Mom is doing all right."

"You knew I would probably faint if I had to change the bandage on Mom's arm," Kristy said.

"It's great that Lisa can stay a while longer to help, but what are we going to do when she has to go home?" Julie said.

"Why are you talking about me like I'm an invalid?" Grandma asked, a little fire returning to her cheeks.

"Mom, you know the doctor said you're to stay off that leg for a week," Lisa reminded her. "A fracture like that doesn't heal overnight."

"It'll be a lot longer than that before you'll be able to climb up in the hay mow or carry hay bales and heavy water buckets," Julie added.

"I don't think it will take me that long to regain my strength," Grandma said, although there was a trace of doubt in her voice.

"The answer seems obvious to me," Lisa said.

Everyone turned to look at her.

"It does?" Grandma said.

"Maybe you're all too close to the situation to see it." She looked toward Kristy. "All I hear from you is how much you want to be out of the city so the girls can enjoy country life, like we did when we were growing up."

Kristy smiled and nodded.

"And Mom, you're always telling me how quiet it is around there, with just that crazy cat of yours for company, and how much you enjoy it when Rosie and Carrie come out."

Grandma nodded.

Julie began to see where Lisa was headed. She looked over at Kristy. "And since you bought Zach, I think you've spent more time at Mom's than you have at your own house."

"Don't you get it yet?" Lisa asked. "Why don't you move in together? It would make it easier for everyone financially too."

Grandma sputtered, "Oh, I'd just be in the way" at the same moment that Kristy blurted, "We really couldn't impose on Mom like that."

Lisa and Julie laughed.

Eric stood up and paced back and forth. "You know, it just might work. That is, if you think you could stand to live with us, Mom."

Grandma's eyes lit up. "Stand it? I'd love it! I never thought you'd want me interfering with your family, that's all."

"If we sold our house, I'd have enough money to add a wing onto yours. You could have your own apartment in case you ever needed to get away from these noisy girls."

For once, the girls weren't being noisy. They had been listening carefully to the conversation. "You mean we'd live with Grandma and the horses and Tick?" Rosie asked.

"And June Bug," Grandma reminded her.

"Oh no, never mind," Eric said with a laugh. "There's no way I could live with that cat."

Rosie and Carrie looked horrified. "Dad!"

"I'm kidding," he assured them.

"Mom, what's wrong?" Kristy sounded alarmed. With all they'd been through that day, this was the first time she had seen tears in her mother's eyes.

"I just can't believe it," Grandma said. "I feel like I'm being adopted too." Kristy gave her a tissue and a hug.

"Well," Lisa announced, "I think this has been enough excitement for Mom for one day. We should get out of here and let her get some rest."

Everyone said their good-byes and quietly left the room.

"Thanks, Lisa," Kristy said.

"For what?"

"For helping us see what was right in front of our eyes."

Lisa smiled. "That's what big sisters are for."

"They're coming!" Rosie said excitedly. She and Carrie had been watching all afternoon for Grandma to arrive from the hospital. They had flipped Carrie's banner from the party over and had written in large letters on the back, "Get Well, Grandma!"

Grandma put her arms around her daughters. They helped her out of the car and into the house. "This is different," she said as she hobbled up the walk. "I'm not used to having people take care of me."

"Surprise!" Rosie and Carrie said in a loud whisper when the front door opened.

"Why are you whispering?" Grandma whispered back.

"You're not going to believe this." Rosie pointed to the corner of the kitchen where Tick and June Bug were curled up side by side, sound asleep.

Grandma stared and shook her head in amazement. "Now *that* is truly a miracle." She stopped to admire the banner the girls had created and made her way to the recliner where she could tilt back and elevate her leg.

"We have this for you." Carrie handed Grandma a bell. "Ring that when you need something, and Rosie and I will come and help you."

"Oh, thank you, Carrie." Grandma looked as if she might start crying, but then the front door flew open. Eric burst into the house, dropping a saddle onto the floor in the entry.

"Woof!" Tick jumped up, and June Bug hissed and swatted at the pup.

"I finally tracked down Kezzie's saddle," Eric announced.

Tick trotted out to the entry and sniffed around the saddle.

"You've been gone long enough," Kristy said. "Where did you find it?"

"First things first. I stopped by the veterinary hospital to pick up Kezzie, but she was starting to have some swelling in her leg."

"Oh! Poor thing," Grandma said.

"They think she's going to be fine, but they want to keep her another day just to be sure."

"She deserves an early retirement," Grandma said. "I'm going to spoil her when she gets back home. Carrie, run and see if your gift is still in the saddlebag."

Carrie rummaged through the pockets. She pulled out two squashed lunch bags and tossed them on the floor. Tick snatched one and ran through the living room with it.

"Oh, get that away from her, Rosie!" Grandma said.

At the bottom of one of the pockets, Carrie found a small, white box, took it out, and handed it to Grandma.

"Oh, good. I was worried it might not be in there." Grandma took the necklace out and fastened it around Carrie's neck. "Happy Adoption Day, Carrie!"

"Oh, Grandma, I love it!"

"The heart is to remind you how much we love you, and the horse represents Zach, your first horse of your very own. You can put two small pictures inside it. I didn't put any in yet because I wanted you to decide which ones you wanted."

"Thank you." Carrie blinked away tears.

Grandma noticed Rosie staring at the necklace. "Don't worry, Rosie. I think you have a birthday coming up, don't you?" She winked at her and Rosie smiled.

Carrie fingered the locket. "I want to put a picture of Mom and Dad on one side and you and Rosie on the other. Thank you so much, Grandma."

Eric waited until they were finished, then cleared his throat. "Umm, Julie, I, uh… I could use your help with something out in the trailer."

"Oh no—what did you do now, Eric?" Kristy asked.

Eric removed his cap and scratched his head. "Well, I called Dr. Rings about picking up the saddle, but she said when she got back to the four-wheeler, the saddle was gone. A guy who lived nearby had seen all the commotion and came to see if he could help. He found the saddle, took it back with him, and left a note with his name and phone number. I contacted him, and when I arrived to pick up the saddle, the guy asked me how Mom and Kezzie were doing." Eric paused and looked around the room.

"And?" Kristy said. "What does all that have to do with whatever is out in the trailer?"

"He started telling me how he had lost his job and his house was in foreclosure. He needed to find a good home for Sassy, and it sounded like Mom was going to need something to ride when her leg healed."

Julie groaned. "Eric! I thought I told you not to buy any more horses without letting me check them out first!"

"I didn't buy her," Eric protested. "He gave her to me. And she's not a horse. She's a mule. I need your help, Julie. She's about kicked the daylights out of that trailer."

Suddenly, they all heard a loud noise—something between a donkey's bray and a wild stallion's bugle, followed by the loud clanging of hooves against metal.

"That's Sassy," Eric said, somewhat regretfully.

Rosie, Carrie, and Grandma looked at each other, then they all burst into laughter.

"This should be interesting," Grandma said.

Chapter 11

Sassy

Rosie jumped to her feet. "I want to see her."

"Me too." Carrie raced after Rosie to the front window. A large, dark brown mule poked her head out the side window of the trailer.

"Wow, look at those ears!" Carrie said.

Grandma reached for her crutches, but Lisa placed her hand firmly on Grandma's shoulder, holding her down in the chair. "Mom, remember? The doctor said you're supposed to stay off that leg for a week."

"Yes, but he didn't know a mule was going to be delivered to my front door!"

"Oh, all right. We'll help you as far as the door so you can take a look at her—*if* you promise to come right back here and rest." Lisa got on one side and Kristy on the other, and they helped Grandma hobble to the entry.

Julie opened the front door and the girls stepped out onto the porch. Sassy brayed again and kicked the side of the trailer impatiently.

"I don't think she likes it in there," Eric said.

"No, I'd say not," Julie agreed. "What have you gotten us into, Eric?"

"Well, it seemed like a good idea at the time. Now, I'm not so sure."

"Oh, she's beautiful!" Grandma exclaimed.

Everyone turned and stared at Sassy. The mule's large head barely fit through the trailer window. Her ears were enormous, and her scraggly tuft of a forelock stood straight up. Lisa shook her head. "Honestly, Mom, only you could think that animal is beautiful. Come on, you better get back inside and prop that leg up."

"Take good care of her. You can put her in the last stall." Grandma reluctantly turned away from the door. "I can't believe I'm missing all the excitement. You girls fill me in on the details after you get her settled in."

Eric looked at Julie. "I'll pull the trailer over to the barn if you'll help me get her out."

The girls hopped into the truck. "We're coming too!"

"I'll go open the gates." Julie headed down the road, unchained the gates to the barn driveway, and propped them open. When Eric had the truck and trailer through, she closed and fastened the gates and followed the trailer to the barn. Eric handed her the lead rope.

"Oh, thanks. What makes you think *I* want to get her out?"

"You're the horse trainer."

"In case you hadn't noticed, this isn't a horse. I've never handled a mule in my life."

"It can't be that much different, can it?"

Sassy brayed again and pawed on the trailer floor.

"I think she wants out, Aunt Julie," Rosie said.

"Uh, yeah, I kind of got that impression too."

"I'll get her out if you don't want to," Eric offered.

"No, no, I can do it."

The next time Sassy poked her head out the trailer window, Julie clipped the lead to her halter and unfastened the trailer tie. "Rosie, open the trailer door enough to let me in so I can get a hold of her."

Rosie ran to the back of the trailer, lifted the latch, and opened the door slightly. Julie slipped through, and Rosie pushed the door shut again. Sassy noticed Julie and started to turn around. She was so large that her head and neck wedged up against the side of the trailer.

"Oh, no!" Julie stared at the mule, wondering what to do.

What's wrong?" Eric asked.

"She's stuck."

Sassy struggled, moving back and forth a little at a time. She finally managed to work herself loose and wound up facing the rear of the trailer.

"There you go," Julie said, relieved. "Now I don't have to back you out." She grabbed the lead rope and patted Sassy's neck. The mule fidgeted nervously, and Julie was careful to keep her feet clear. "Rosie, open the door wide and stay out of the way. She may come out in a hurry!"

Rosie opened the door as far as it would go and stood behind it. Carrie ran to join her, and they peeked around the corner.

Julie stepped forward. The large mule saw daylight where the closed door had been, and her big, furry ears flicked forward. She stepped to the end of the trailer, put her head down, and sniffed around. Cautiously, she stepped off the edge with one front foot, then the other. Soon all four hooves were on solid ground.

"Good girl." Julie praised her and relaxed a little. Maybe this wasn't going to be so difficult after all. Sassy walked to the edge of the drive and began to graze on a few clumps of grass. Suddenly, Scamper and Zach, at the back of the pasture, spotted the trailer. Apparently thinking their friend, Kezzie, had returned, they whinnied and galloped toward the barn. Sassy jerked her head up and started toward the pasture gate to meet them.

Julie clamped down on the lead and gave a jerk. "Whoa, big girl." The mule paid no attention and began trotting, dragging Julie behind her. "Whoa, I said!" Julie yelled, yanking the lead in a desperate attempt to stop her, but by then Sassy had broken into a canter. Julie dropped the lead rope and watched helplessly as the mule ran off to join the horses.

Eric and the girls ran to catch up with Julie. "Are you okay?" he asked.

"Yeah, I'm fine. I think we just invented a new sport—mule skiing. You know, being dragged along behind a mule. Wow, is she ever strong!"

"I didn't think about the other horses being out," Eric said.

Sassy pranced up and down the fence line, squealing and grunting at the horses. Zach and Scamper seemed surprised to see a long-eared distant relative rather than Kezzie. They soon lost interest and returned to their grazing. Sassy stood with her head over the fence, gazing longingly at them.

Julie walked up to her and picked up the lead rope. "I can see I have a lot of work to do with you, big girl." Sassy rubbed her head against Julie's shoulder, knocking her backwards. "Oh no, you don't. You're too big for that kind of stuff. I know you're trying to be friendly, but you're not allowed to push me."

She corrected Sassy with a sharp snap on the lead rope. Sassy looked surprised, and turned her big, sad eyes to Julie as if to say, "Why'd you do that? I just want to be your friend."

"She's huge," Carrie said. "She looks like she's going to have a baby."

"I think it might be twins," Rosie added.

Julie laughed. "Mules can't have babies, but yeah, she apparently has a healthy appetite."

Rosie pointed toward Sassy's feet. "Look at her hooves. They're all chipped and cracked."

"That's odd. Mules are known for having strong hooves." Julie looked closer at Sassy's feet and frowned. Each hoof had large chunks broken out of it. "Rosie, do you know when Dean is scheduled to trim the horses' hooves again?"

"No, but he just did them before the fair, so it will probably be a while."

"We'll have to get him to come out before then. She needs something done to these hooves right away. And she's going to need a new halter."

Carrie looked at Sassy's multicolored, neon halter. "Don't you like the colors of this one? I think it looks neat."

"It's not the colors. In fact, it looks like it might glow in the dark. That might come in handy—we could be sure we'd never lose her," Julie laughed. "The problem is that I don't have any control of her with this flat nylon halter. When I pulled on her to stop, she didn't even feel it. She needs a rope halter, maybe with a couple of knots over the nose—something that will get her attention."

"Oh," Carrie said. "I didn't know there was any other kind of halter."

"I'll bring one from home tomorrow. Let's see if we can get her in the barn now."

Carrie and Rosie ran to open the barn and stall doors. Julie started for the barn, and Sassy calmly followed.

"She seems okay now," Eric said.

"Yeah, I have a feeling that as long as we're doing what Sassy wants to do, she's fine. She needs to learn to do what I want her to do." Julie led her into the stall and unfastened the lead. Rosie ran to get a flake of hay, and Carrie grabbed the hose to fill her water bucket.

When she was settled in, they all stood outside the stall, watching her. Sassy circled around, checking everything out, then began to nibble on her hay.

"From what the guy told me, no one has paid much attention to her for several years," Eric said.

"It shows," Julie said. "You girls stay away from her until I've had a chance to work with her. I don't think she's mean. She's just very large and has no manners. She might hurt you accidentally."

"Did you two hear what Julie said?" Eric asked.

The girls nodded.

"I didn't plan to get close to her anyway," Carrie said.

Rosie looked doubtful. "Do you think Grandma's going to be able to ride her? I don't want her to get hurt again."

"I'll know more when I've ridden her myself. She may be fine under saddle," Julie said.

"Mules are very sure-footed. She should be great for trail rides," Eric added.

"She obviously wasn't being well cared for, so like Bandit—I mean, Zach—she's kind of a rescue project. If I keep working with her, I should have her behaving by the time Mom's leg is healed. Then she can decide whether she wants to ride her or not. Who knows? Maybe I'll like her so much, I'll keep her for myself."

"Do you need anything else, Aunt Julie?" Rosie asked. "I want to go tell Grandma about Sassy."

"Have her call Dean and get an appointment set up. I'll be back tomorrow to throw a saddle on Sassy and see how she rides."

Rosie tugged on Carrie's sleeve, and they raced out of the barn to report back to Grandma.

Chapter 12
The Opportunity

Carrie and Zach had a clean round so far in the Olympic competition. She focused her attention on the last jump—a 1.6-meter triple oxer. It looked awfully high, but she was confident Zach could handle it. She squeezed her heels, urging him forward, and he responded immediately.

A loud clanging sound suddenly caused Zach to shy and bolt off course. "No, boy, no!" Carrie fought desperately to steer him back in line with the jump. The noise grew louder and louder. Zach began to fade away underneath her. Now she was on foot, running toward the jump herself. "No!" she shouted. "I can't make it." She trembled with fear.

"Hey." Rosie shook Carrie gently. "Wake up."

"No! I can't jump it!" Carrie yelled.

"What in the world are you talking about?" Rosie laughed as Carrie blinked her eyes and looked around the room.

"Oh, I guess it was a dream." Carrie's fogginess began to clear, and she remembered that they had spent the night at Grandma's so they could help take care of her.

"Come on. Grandma's ringing her bell. She needs us for something."

Carrie crawled out of bed and followed Rosie downstairs to Grandma's room.

She was sitting up in bed, looking much more chipper than the day before. "Good morning, girls. I thought you two were going to sleep all day."

Rosie looked at the clock on the wall. "Umm, Grandma, it's only nine o'clock."

"Oh, really? It seems much later. I slept so much in the hospital, I'm not tired. After you eat your breakfast, maybe we could play a game of Horse-opoly. I hear Carrie's quite good at it."

Rosie grinned. "Okay, Grandma, that sounds like fun."

The girls hurried off to the kitchen, where Kristy and Lisa were having coffee. Kristy looked up as the girls entered. "Grab a bowl of cereal and join us. Did you two sleep well?"

"I slept like a log," Rosie replied. "But Carrie was having a crazy dream. She was talking in her sleep too." Rosie repeated in a high, squeaky voice. "No! No! I can't jump it!"

Carrie laughed. "Zach and I were close to winning the Olympics—until Grandma's bell scared him."

"Yeah, right. If anyone wins the Olympics, it will be Scamper," Rosie insisted.

"Sit down and eat," Kristy said. "Don't you two ever get tired of arguing?"

Rosie gave her an odd look. "We're not arguing, Mom."

"Oh? What do you call it then?"

Rosie looked at Carrie. "Debating?"

Carrie shook her head. When she had finished chewing a bite of cereal, she said, "Discussing."

"Well, that's good—I guess. It always sounds like arguing to me." Kristy took her coffee cup to the sink and glanced out the back window.

"When you're done eating, let Tick out of her pen and take care of the horses. Julie will be here in a while to look after Sassy."

"Okay, then we're going to play Horse-opoly with Grandma," Carrie said.

"Good," Lisa said. "She's only been home a day, and she's already restless. You girls are going to have your hands full keeping her entertained."

Just then the front door flew open, and Julie ran through it, waving a piece of paper. "You guys aren't going to believe this! This is such an incredible opportunity. I can't believe it!"

"Hi, Julie. How are you this morning?" Kristy said. "Nice of you to drop in."

"No, seriously, you won't believe it. Where's Mom? And Eric? They need to hear this!"

"Take some deep breaths and calm down before you hyperventilate," Lisa said. "We'll go get Mom. Girls, go get your dad. I think he's out back chopping firewood."

Soon they were all gathered around the kitchen table. Julie slapped the paper down on the middle of the table, making the girls jump. "This is our answer," she announced.

Everyone looked around at each other and then back at Julie, unsure what the question was to which she had discovered the answer. Grandma picked up the paper and examined it. "An auction?"

"Yep. It's a horse farm. It's been abandoned for several years. The bank finally foreclosed on it, and it's up for sale at auction."

"And… what does this have to do with us?" Eric asked.

"We're going to buy it."

"We are?" Kristy said blankly.

"Yes, all of us. You were going to sell your house anyway and move in with Mom, right?"

Kristy and Eric nodded.

"Well, if Mom sells this place, then you could all move to the new farm."

"Why would we do that?" Grandma asked.

"Oh, where do I start?" Julie asked. "Let's see… there's one hundred acres. The property is beautiful, and the indoor arena is about three times the size of mine."

"Indoor arena?" Grandma perked up. "Tell us more."

"Did I mention it's two miles from our house, down a quiet country road? The kids could ride their bikes, or the horses, back and forth."

Rosie and Carrie were beginning to catch Julie's enthusiasm. The idea of being close to their cousins was exciting, and the indoor arena was almost beyond their dreams.

"The barn has twenty-five stalls. I could expand my training and lesson business, and we could take on a few boarders to help cover expenses."

"Okay, what's the catch?" Eric asked. "One hundred acres, twenty-five stalls, indoor riding arena. How could we possibly afford it?"

"Well, the house is a little run-down," Julie admitted.

"How run-down?" Eric asked suspiciously.

"I don't think anyone's lived there for at least five years, but I'm sure we can get it cheap, and with your building experience, I know you could fix it up."

"Yeah, Dad, and we'll help you," Rosie said.

Julie looked over at Lisa. "You're welcome to join us. There will be plenty of room for everyone."

Lisa considered it. "It's awfully tempting, but I'm not sure I could convince Robert to leave Texas. I'll bet Lauren would love to spend a few months with you each summer, though."

"Wow, this sounds even better than Cousins Camp!" Carrie said.

Julie looked around. She could see everyone was warming to the idea. "Well, what do you think, Mom?"

Grandma picked up the auction paper and slowly read over it again. "The auction is in three weeks. Why don't we go take a look at it soon? Then we can decide whether we want to bid on it."

"Yahoo!" the girls jumped out of their seats, giving each other high fives.

"Don't get too excited," Grandma warned. "Even if we do like it and try to buy it, we might get outbid."

That possibility did little to dampen the girls' or Julie's enthusiasm. "All right, you two, are you ready to help me train a mule? Let's head over to the barn."

Book 3: Clothed With Thunder

If you liked the first two books in the Sonrise Stable series, be sure to read more about the family's adventures in *Clothed With Thunder.*

When a fellow 4-H member gives a presentation on the evolution of the horse, Rosie and Carrie are determined to prove to the club members that horses did not evolve, but were created by God.

Grandma is forced to the sidelines for a time as she and Kezzie recover from their trail riding accident. Is Julie able to train Sassy? Will the family purchase the new riding stable with the indoor arena that Grandma has always dreamed about?

The Sonrise Stable Series

Book 1: Rosie and Scamper

Book 2: Carrie and Bandit

Book 3: Clothed with Thunder

Book 4: Tender Mercies

Book 5: Outward Appearances

Book 6: Coming in 2014—Follow Our Leader

Available at sonrisestable.com & love2ridehorses.com

For as many as are led by the Spirit of God, these are sons of God. For you did not receive the spirit of bondage again to fear, but you received the Spirit of adoption by whom we cry out, "Abba, Father." The Spirit himself bears witness with our spirit that we are children of God, and if children, then heirs—heirs of God and joint heirs with Christ...

Romans 8:14-17

Just as Carrie was chosen and adopted by Rosie's parents, and learned to call them "Mom and Dad," so we are chosen by God to become His children. As children of God, we are allowed to call the Creator of the universe "Abba, Father." Although it wasn't required because of Carrie's age, the judge asked her if she wanted to be adopted, and Carrie said "Yes."

We all have a similar choice to make. Will we accept God as our Father, or will we rebelliously go our own way? Just as it was for Carrie, the choice should be an easy one. Why would anyone not want to be a child of the one true God and inherit eternal life?

When I was young, a neighbor, Bill Steffens, was a strong influence in my life. My dad traded him my wild pony, Cricket, and a pig for one of his well-trained ponies, named Dolly. He taught me a lot about horses and how to ride. His involvement in my life helped a shy, insecure girl begin to feel worthwhile.

Bill and his wife adopted four young children and were foster parents to a boy my own age. Their example helped me, later in life, to understand the concept of our adoption into God's family. I pray that this book will help you understand also and will bring you closer to the decision to become a child of God.

The Difficult to Catch Horse: A Training Tip from Lynn Baber

Cleveland Amory's book, *Ranch of Dreams*, includes the story of a doctor who owned a horse named Cody. Cody would not come to his owner when called, but he would come when his caretaker called him. This so infuriated the doctor that he shot the horse in the knee. The doctor was fined, but a judge refused to have the horse taken away from him. The doctor later sold Cody at an auction. He likely would have ended up at a slaughterhouse if a rescue group hadn't heard about it and purchased him. Cody spent the rest of his life in peace and safety at Amory's ranch.

Difficulty in catching horses is common; however, there are safe and effective techniques you can learn to avoid or eliminate the problem. Were you surprised by the strategy Julie used to catch Bandit in the book? The approach was based on advice from trainer Lynn Baber.

Here's what Lynn has to say on the topic:

Every horse who refuses to be caught is unwilling, whether from fear, a misplaced sense of fun, or a lack of respect. Julie exhibited understanding of Bandit's equine nature by offering leadership and building a relationship instead of simply trying to "catch" him. You catch a fish, but you build a relationship with a horse.

Chasing a horse is always a sign of weakness, and it will increase the horse's level of fear or power. Teach your horse to come when called, or at the very least, to politely stand still when you put on a halter or loop a lead rope around his or her neck. Horses who respect their owners are happier and more secure than those who don't.

When you bring home a new horse, the best thing to do is to limit its freedom until your relationship is established. Horses gain confidence in routine. New horses need to know that food and water will arrive regularly and which faces are friendly. Provide a routine before you teach other lessons. Would you really be able to concentrate on your teacher if the first week of school was held next to the roller coaster at an amusement park? Limiting the freedom of your horse places a limit on possible distractions. Because you need your horse's full attention, don't turn him out with other horses at first.

If your new horse already has good manners, make his first home a stall until he knows the routine. Lead him around to see his new home, hear new noises, see new sights, and spend time getting to know you. Turn your horse out for stress-free exercise in a small area to speed up the period of adjustment. If possible, get your horse out every few hours. Soon he will begin looking for you and greet you when you enter the barn.

If your new horse is fearful or hard to catch, make his or her first home a small round pen. A stall would be too stressful, a paddock too big. The first stage of teaching a horse to come to you is getting his attention and having control of his feet.

Once your new horse is in a stall or small pen, you will feed, clean, and spend time around your horse just as Carrie did. Concentrate on the task and not on the horse. Of course, you must always be aware of what your horse is doing, so you don't get stepped on or run over.

Sometimes horses just need to touch you first. When his soft nose touches you for the first time, calmly look at him as if to say, "Oh, hello. I didn't even know you were here." Then take your attention away again. The concepts presented in *Carrie and Bandit* apply whether your horse is in a stall or in a pasture.

When approaching new horses, always move toward their withers. Walk calmly, but don't sneak. Stop every few strides to look around as if you don't even see the horse. Walk forward again. Repeat this until you are next to the horse. Success is reaching out a hand to softly pet your horse on the withers; then turn and walk away. You are teaching your horse that you won't hurt him and you aren't there to simply catch a fish.

Spend time with your horse having fun. If you only catch your horse to work him or do lessons, he'll see no benefit to being haltered, and you'll start down the wrong road again. Horses understand friendship and family. Be a good friend and a good leader and your horse will start waiting for you at the gate.

Lynn's book, *Amazing Grays, Amazing Grace*, explores the many ways our relationships with our horses are similar to our relationship with God. Learn more about Lynn Baber, her books, and her approach to horse training at her website, lynnbaber.com.

Lost Acres Horse Rescue and Rehabilitation

For those who love horses, it's difficult to imagine how someone *(like the doctor who shot Cody or the fictional Billy King in the Sonrise Stable books)* could deliberately harm a horse. It's encouraging to know that some abused and neglected horses eventually find a place of refuge and safety at one of the many horse rescues across the country, such as Lost Acres Horse Rescue and Rehabilitation in Chillicothe, Ohio. At these rescues, they are treated with love and respect—maybe for the first time in their lives.

LAHRR, founded by Sissy Burggraf in 1994, has provided help and a home for more than one hundred horses. In Sissy's eyes, every horse is a champion. Each horse that arrives at Lost Acres has fought his most gallant battle and won… the battle for life!

Sissy could fill a book with stories of the horses she has rescued over the years. Here, she describes two of her champions: Ginger and Sandy.

Ginger

When Gwen* discovered Ginger lying by a fence, unable to get up, she tracked down the owner to see whether he would be willing to sell her. The man asked how much she would give for the almost lifeless horse. Checking her pockets, Gwen came up with ten dollars. "SOLD!" the man responded. As they used a tractor to lift Ginger off the ground, he explained how they had ridden the horse every day—until she went down and refused to get up.

Words can't begin to describe Ginger's condition. She had the equivalent of bedsores on each hip area, so deep the muscles were coming through. She had a severe ulceration on her chest and another nearly to the bone on her right knee. Her front suspensories were so swollen and torn that they were basically "mush." Ginger's feet were infected with thrush and stuck out to the front as she used her ankles to walk. Skin was beginning to slough off her legs, and her chest was swollen with accumulating fluid. She was also six hundred pounds underweight.

Why did we not euthanize her immediately? Despite all this, Ginger had the most beautiful copper-colored coat, the clearest, brightest eyes full of light, and the biggest will to live that I have ever seen in a horse.

When Gwen brought Ginger to us, I explained that I wasn't worried much about the sores on her body or the weight loss. My biggest fear was what would happen when she began gaining weight. Would her legs be able to support her?

I worked with Ginger feverishly day after day— bathing, treating, and bandaging her wounds. Her chest was lanced to clear the fluid. After several weeks, her knee and chest began to heal, and the thrush was completely gone. The swelling began to subside from her suspensories, and soon she was able to walk upright on her feet. We fought abscesses and overcame those. Despite all the problems Ginger had encountered, nothing had affected her appetite. She ate like three horses and began to gain weight—and more weight.

Although she had recovered in so many ways, her weight would prove to be her tragic end. A little over a year later, Ginger had gained five hundred pounds, and her weakened legs could no longer carry her. Not wanting her to suffer or endure more pain than she already had, she was humanely euthanized by our veterinarian and buried on our farm.

* name changed

Sandy

As with many of our rescues, it started with a phone call. Would we accept Sandy, a seventeen-year-old Arabian? Sandy had escaped from an unlatched stall and was poisoned after gorging on hog feed.

When we arrived to pick her up, Sandy was curled into a fetal position from chemical poisoning. She pulled herself along the ground with her front feet as she attempted to care for her six-month-old foal. Encounters with the electric fence had resulted in burns on her mouth and tongue. We were informed that Sandy had been down for a week, but the ulcers on her elbows, stomach, and legs indicated she had lain there much longer.

Space does not permit me to tell Sandy's entire story, but because of her will and courage, I feel it's important to relate some of the things this brave horse endured. The bulbs of her heels blew out due to infection. She lost the soles of her feet and began to literally lose her hooves, which would flop up and down as she walked. We scooted Sandy from side to side in her stall to clean it. A month passed before she could get up and down on her own. The vet warned us that, even with all our love and care, euthanasia might be inevitable for Sandy.

After eighteen long months, the day came for the big test: Sandy's first turnout in the pasture. As I released the lead rope, she looked from side to side and smelled the air.

Tears streamed down my face as I watched LAHRR's "miracle baby." She raced around the large field, her mane and tail blowing in the wind, whinnying at the top of her voice with every lap.

Sandy fully recovered and was adopted as a riding horse by a wonderful family. They kept Sandy until she passed away at the ripe old age of twenty-seven.

Lost Acres no longer offers horses for adoption. Each horse that enters their facility is loved and cared for at LAHRR for the remainder of his or her life. LAHRR is able to provide shelter for these horses through tax-deductible donations.

For more information about what they offer and how you can help, visit their website at www.lostacresrescue.org.

CPSIA information can be obtained
at www.ICGtesting.com
Printed in the USA
FFOW01n1333301215
20061FF

9 780984 724215